THE QUILT TRILOGY
THE
BLUE DOOR

THE QUILT TRILOGY
THE
BLUE DOOR

ANN RINALDI

SCHOLASTIC PRESS ᕲᨆᨆᨆᕲ NEW YORK

YA

Library of Congress Cataloging-in-Publication Data

Rinaldi, Ann.
The blue door / Ann Rinaldi.
p.   cm. — (The quilt trilogy ; #3)
Summary: When her grandmother sends her alone on a difficult
journey up North, fourteen-year-old Amanda encounters the
exploitation of women in textile mills.
ISBN 0-590-46051-X
[1. Grandmothers—Fiction.   2. Women textile workers—Fiction.]
I. Title.   II. Series: Rinaldi, Ann. Quilt trilogy ; #3.
PZ7.R459B1   1996
[Fic]—dc20   95-39318
CIP
AC

12 11 10 9 8 7 6 5 4 3 2 1   6 7 8 9/9 0 1/0

Printed in the U.S.A.   37

First printing, September 1996

The type in this book was set in Goudy Old Style.

In Memory of my Aunt Margaret
who gave me my start

The Chelmsford Family

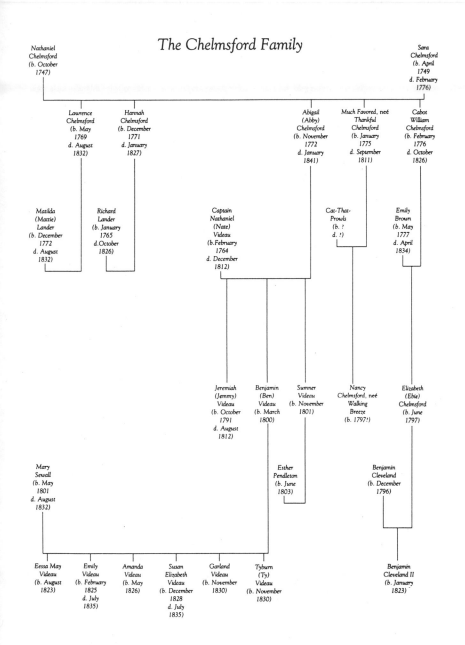

THE QUILT TRILOGY
THE
BLUE DOOR

Chapter One

December 1840

I talk too much, there's my problem. Grandmother Abigail says it's in the blood, but I should still try to curb the habit. Daddy doesn't say much about it at all. Half the time he has spells of deafness. Comes from when Doctor Fripp gave him too much quinine for a fever and left him deaf as a teaspoon for days.

I've always liked to talk. In our house there are too many silences. And they're as deep as the tides around here at the time of the new or full moon. You could drown in them. So I talk.

But it gets me in trouble. Like the time I said at supper, "Daddy got more than four hundred turtle eggs today on the beach."

My daddy loves hunting for turtle eggs. But that did it for Daphne, my stepmother. She was livid.

"Getting down on your hands and knees in the mud is not suitable recreation, Ben," she said.

Daphne is very high-toned. Daddy says she can't help it, she's from Charleston. "It's nigra work," she scolded, "what will people think?"

You see? I was just making conversation and I got Daddy in trouble. Then I went and got myself in trouble. Everybody said I'd do that sooner or later.

I made mention of the unmentionable in our house. That Daphne is addicted to opium.

Twice each lunar day the tide flows toward the land here on St. Helena's Island. Then it flows back to the sea.

Twice each lunar day, Daphne fills up with anger, either at one of us or one of the negroes. And when her anger dies down, she's like the mudflats after the tide goes out. Friendly only to oyster catchers and hungry crabs.

It's the opium. She's either going uphill or down-dale from it. Everybody knows it. But it's one of those things we have a code of silence about here. Like the fact that Daddy's brother, Sumner, has no luck hunting and has never been able to bag a deer.

But I broke the code. I not only made mention of the fact that Daphne is addicted to opium. I also threw the words right in her face.

That was when Grandmother Abigail asked me if I could keep silent for two weeks. Not talk at all.

"Not talk for two weeks?" I could scarce believe what I was hearing.

"It's a challenge, Amanda," she said. "Like when your father goes through the actions of preparing for a duel. He does it because he's been challenged."

"He doesn't duel anymore," I told her.

"Exactly. Because it is no longer necessary to exchange pistol shots to give satisfaction to an injured party. But the challenge is delivered. Your father accepts it. Then he engages a second, sets a time and place. And the injured party makes public his grievances. And the social balance is restored."

Grandmother is very taken with social balance. Still, I was confused. "You mean you're just *challenging* me to stay silent for two weeks? And I don't really have to do it?"

"No, Amanda, in this case you must do it," she said sadly.

"Why?"

"Because by doing so you will help the injured party."

"I don't care about Daphne. I hate her," I said.

To give her credit, she didn't take on about my hating. She stayed unruffled. "The injured party is yourself, Amanda. You talk too much. There may come a time when your tongue gets you into real trouble. Or when your silence keeps you out of it. The time has come to see if you have any character."

Character is important to Grandmother.

"Only my first son had it," she told me. "It's my fault your daddy and your uncle Sumner don't have it. I spoiled them so much after Jemmy was killed, fighting in the last war."

"My daddy's a good man," I told her.

She sniffed. "Yes, he is. A dear man. But he is intemperate, cocky, inadequate, and a spend-thrift. He is land and slave rich without a dollar in his pocket. But his worst sin is that he married outside the family circle. Twice."

There wasn't much I could say to that. It was all true.

Grandmother has character, enough for us all.

"Of course, I have faults, too," she admitted. "I don't like to pay my bills. I live off my capital, not my income, my plantations are undercultivated and too many of my people are idle."

And you're married to a no-count scoundrel, I thought. But then, I suppose when you get to be seventy and have been a belle in your early years and are on your third husband, when you own four plantations and two-hundred and fifty negroes, you can make the rules.

You can even ask your granddaughter if she will stay silent for two weeks. And have her do it.

All this happened in December of 1840, right after Daddy's creditors came to Yamassee, our plantation, under court judgment, to take six of his servants for nonpayment of debt.

It was a cold December morning a week before Christmas when our servants were taken. We were at breakfast, I and my brothers, Ty and Garland, who are twins, ten years old, and the plague of St. Helena's Parish. And my sister Eessa May who is seventeen and so tainted with vanity that even when she is eating with the family, she is looking around to see who is admiring her.

The trouble with Eessa May is they named her after the plantation. Her name is Yamassee spelled backwards, a strange enough name frontwards. You can't help but be tainted with vanity, I suppose, when you're named after 376 acres of improved and unimproved land.

Daphne was at breakfast, too. Daphne is also our aunt because she was Mama's sister before Mama died.

Daddy was grumpy because his second cousin, "the Major," was coming over and the haunch of venison he wanted to give him was missing. It's a matter of prestige that a man be able to give gifts to friends and relatives.

"Rob Roy took it, I'll wager," Daphne said. "That man's a born thief."

"Rob Roy doesn't need to take it. I'd give it to him if he wanted it," Daddy said. Rob Roy was his driver, his overseer, and his mainstay. He freed Daddy up from having to supervise things in the fields.

"The dogs took it," Eessa May said. "I saw them with it last night."

Now who's talking too much, I wondered.

"That's just as bad," Daphne insisted. "It's that fool Melody. You ought to destroy her."

"No!" Garland glared at her.

"She's my best dog for the hunt," Daddy said.

"Well then, you'll have to drown some of her pups. We've enough dogs on this place."

"Dad-*dee*!" Garland begged.

"I'll give them to the Major. The only reason he wants to hunt with me is because of my dogs." Daddy laughed.

Daphne didn't. "Well then, send them. Or I'll drown them myself."

I don't know what all would have happened if Rob Roy hadn't stood in the doorway then. "Suh."

"Come on in," Daddy said as he did every morning.

"Must that uppity nigra be at my breakfast?" Daphne whispered as she did every morning.

Rob Roy came in. He didn't walk, or slouch, like the other negroes. He strode. He had very long legs and he dressed well, in Daddy's castoffs. He had a narrow waist and broad shoulders. He carried his head high. "Six horses down with the distemper, suh."

"Who?"

"Puss, Dutchess, Isaac, Prince, Hyder, and Fanny."

"Black Hawk?" Daddy asked.

"He be fine, suh."

"You know what to do, Rob Roy. Smoke them up the nostrils with tar, pine tops, feathers, and powdered sulfur."

"Yessuh."

"Has the wind damaged anything?" The wind had blown hard all night.

"Some of the new orange trees down. Some fences."

"Set the hands to picking cotton."

"Yessuh."

"And Rob Roy," Daddy said as he was leaving the room.

"Yessuh?"

"Have the negroes in the front yard at eleven. That's when Mr. Tribley comes."

The tall, gentle overseer who'd been with us for ten years looked sad for a moment. "How many goes, suh?"

"Six."

"Who?"

"My wife has made up the list. She'll give it to Mr. Tribley. Can't be helped, Rob Roy. I'm sorry."

"Will they be stayin' in the lowcountry, suh? They be wantin' to know."

"Can't say, Rob Roy. Sorry."

The man left. I saw Daphne smiling. There was a strange glint of satisfaction in her eyes. And it was then that I knew Rob Roy's name was on the list.

I got my hands on her list after breakfast. Being fourteen, I still go to school in the village every day with my brothers. But it had closed early for the Christmas holiday because of a spread of "hot fever."

Daphne had retired to her room, likely to take her daily dose of opium, with molasses and aromatic barks in it, for a "nervous disorder."

I brought her some coffee on a tray. She was lying down. She drank gallons of coffee every day, with the milk boiled in it just right, all frothy on top. If the milk wasn't frothy, she went into a frenzy with the negro who was unlucky enough to serve her.

She had all the negroes running to do her bidding, fetching her sketching materials, her coffee, and her ice, with which she fought the heat in summer.

Daddy keeps us at Yamassee in the summer to save on expenses, though many other families go north, some to Saratoga. We ward off the summer fever with quinine and ice, 125 pounds of it a week, over from Beaufort.

I set the coffee down on a table. "Thank you, Amanda. How nice."

She was uphill already from the opium, I could tell by the slur in her voice. She never took notice as I stopped at her vanity table on the way out. The list was there. I ran my eyes down it quickly.

There was his name. Rob Roy. I ran from the room.

Daddy was gone. Lavinia, in the kitchen, told me he was out on Black Hawk, seeing what fences had been damaged.

I ran outside. The wind was still blowing and the sand with it. Sand got in my eyes and ears and stung my face as I ran out back, on the land side of the house, through the yard and down a path to the quarters and workhouses concealed by trees and shrubs.

Rob Roy was coming out of the toolhouse. I ran to him.

"Your name! It's on the list!"

He dropped a hammer and sack of nails. The wind blew off his hat and he didn't even bother to pick it up.

"I knowed she would do it. She hates me, 'cause I can read and write."

"She hates you, because you're the only servant who won't lose his dignity to her."

Wind tore at my hair, whipped my skirts. Tore the words from my mouth.

"He won't let me go," Rob Roy said.

"He won't be able to help it. He can't go against her. Never will. You've got to run, Rob Roy. Now. You've got an hour before Mr. Tribley comes. Please!"

He looked around him. No one was about. The other negroes were in the fields. He nodded, reached out, and touched my shoulder. "Thank you, Miss Amanda. I be back in a few days. Will you tell my June?"

"Yes." June worked in the house, as seamstress.

Then he walked to his cabin. It was made of

rough board siding. But the door and window frames were painted blue to keep out "hants."

Hants are ghosts or bad spirits. All the negro cabins in the lowcountry have blue doors and windows. I'd wanted Daddy to paint our door blue, too. We have too many hants in our house for my liking. I think he would have, but Daphne forbade it. What can you expect from somebody who comes from Charleston?

I knew it would be all right if Rob Roy ran. Slaves ran all the time on St. Helena's Island. Some to the woods for a few days for a breather, some to see their families on nearby plantations.

All Daddy's runaways came back. Daddy sold one named January out of the district for running too often. January crept back into our kitchen one night and asked to be bought back.

And Daddy sends Rob Roy to Grandmother's on the mainland all the time, on errands. I went into the house, telling myself it would be all right.

At eleven o'clock, Daddy stood in the front yard, looking downcast as one of his hound dogs who'd just chased a deer into the ocean and seen it drown. Ty and Garland stood next to him. They may be only ten, but they knew it was their place to do so.

"Well, I didn't think Ben would have the gumption to come back and face this," Daphne said.

I was standing on the upstairs gallery. She came

up behind me, looking triumphant, nothing less.

Mr. Tribley, of Tribley, Oakes, and Dresser, had her list. He read the names off it.

"Peggy, Darcy, Belinda," he called out.

The wind had died down and it had gotten cold. You could see Tribley's breath in the air. And feel the anguish, like the biting cold.

The names sounded like a death knell. Behind me, Daphne moved, standing on tiptoe.

"Where is Rob Roy?" she hissed.

I didn't answer.

There were cries, moanings, lamentations, as the first three servants stepped out of line. "Please don't send me, Master, please!" Peggy was begging.

Daddy just turned away.

Then, from Mr. Tribley: "Jodine, April, Rob Roy."

Two more stepped out. Jodine and April.

"Where is Rob Roy?" Daphne grabbed my arm. "Where *is* he?"

"How would I know?" I asked.

"You've warned him," she hissed. "He isn't here, is he? You saw my list. That's why you brought coffee to my room. Then you ran down to the quarters to warn him. And now he's gone."

"If he is, it's a good thing," I said.

"Your father will hear of this."

"He can't do without Rob Roy. The man can

read and figure. He can track the rows of corn and weigh the cotton. He carries out Daddy's written instructions."

"Your father will *hear* of this. You'll be punished."

"He saved Daddy's life that time their skiff overturned on the river."

Daphne was tall, thin, and aristocratic. I think she married my father to make him miserable. She said once that his indifference "killed my sister." She hated me. Likely because she could not make me lose my dignity. Like Rob Roy.

"You will be punished," she said again. It was a promise.

I wanted to sass her about her opium-taking then and there, but I didn't. I held my tongue and met her cold blue stare. "You can't separate a slave from his wife," I said. "The Savannah River Baptist Association says separating families is the civil equivalent of death."

"You don't even know what that means."

"Yes I do."

"We're Episcopal, not Baptist."

"Reverend McElheran said it in church."

"Insolence." She raised her cane. She always used a cane. She said it gave her authority with the negroes. Frequently she hit them with it when they didn't fetch her opium fast enough.

I stood my ground. I would not let her frighten me.

"You're as insolent as your grandmother. She's never respected me. Go from my sight!"

I walked the gallery all around the house. I could see south, across at least three miles of marsh islands and mudflats, now under water. There on Station Creek, almost out to Bay Point, was a raft being poled by a man.

Rob Roy, on his way up to Broad River and Beaufort on a rising tide.

Just below me I saw Mr. Tribley and his men leading six of our negroes to the dock. I was shocked to see that now Rodney was one of them. He was elderly. I felt bad. But Daddy *needed* Rob Roy more than he needed Rodney. Peggy, wrists bound, turned to plead with Daddy to save her.

He stood there on the grassy slope that led to the dock, saying nothing, affecting disinterest. With Daddy, once his cotton was sold, he did not ask what became of it. And now he was treating his negroes the same way.

To satisfy Daphne I wasn't allowed to go to Beaufort with Daddy on Saturday. I always went with him; while he settled his accounts with shop owners, visited his lawyer, saddler, or gunsmith, I'd buy confections or go to the bookstore. We'd get the mail and packages of goods on the wharf, delivered by steamship from Charleston, and stop in to see Grandmother.

My deprivation seemed to satisfy Daphne. And

by Christmas she forgot her complaints about "that uppity negro, Rob Roy, who was still skulking about this place." Rob Roy had come back.

I suspect that Daddy was secretly beholden to me for warning Rob Roy. He brought me back some sweets, and a book from Beaufort.

Chapter Two

Christmas morning the weather turned so cold that icicles a foot long hung on the pump. So cold we did not go to church. The wild ducks left the ponds and took to the woods and rushes.

Daddy and Daphne had hosted a party on Christmas Eve and Ty and Garland had come down with the fever right in the middle of it. Daddy sat up most of the night with them.

At breakfast on Christmas Daddy looked spent. He ate just dark coffee and a biscuit. Then he took *The Planter's Guide and Family Book of Medicine* down from the shelf and went into the kitchen. The book was fat, old, and worn. And Daddy only took it down when things got serious.

We heard him in the kitchen with Lavinia, asking for some of her decoctions. And we knew he was rolling some pills. Lavinia was keeper of the grasses and herbs, the fever root, powdered fruit rinds, pastes, teas, powders, and salves for our medicines, all gotten from the woods and fields.

Eessa and I stuffed ourselves silly with oranges and cake from Grandmother, then went to the sitting room to open our presents in front of the roaring fire.

Daddy gave me *The Vicar of Wakefield* by Oliver Goldsmith. And a fine lace collar and a bag of sweets. He gave Eessa a gold breast pin and a velvet cape.

Daphne came in with a glass of champagne. "Play the violin, Eessa," she said.

So Eessa played some Christmas music. In the kitchen the servants were assembling to put together dinner. Wild turkey, venison, turtle soup. I felt good, though a little worried about my brothers. Outside the wind howled, but we were warm and safe.

In a little while Daddy went upstairs. He came back down and I heard him talking with Rob Roy in the hall. Then Daddy came into the room, carrying some blue pills on a plate. He held them out to us.

"No," Eessa set down her violin. "I won't take them. They make me dizzy. Vile things. And you know John's coming for supper."

"I don't want my girls sick," Daddy said. "I've given the boys twenty grains each." His eyes were pleading.

"Daddy, you've an irrational terror of illness!" Eessa stamped across the room. "You make us all crazy with it. Daphne, tell him I don't need his silly blue pills!"

Daphne had been lounging in a chair with her eyes closed. Now she opened them, got up and walked languidly to the window to feed her pet bird in its cage. Just then Rob Roy galloped by outside, the horse's hooves sounding on the frozen ground.

"Why are you allowing that uppity nigra to ride Black Hawk?" Daphne asked Daddy.

"He's fetching Doctor Fripp for the boys."

I felt a knell in my bones. Daddy seldom sent for a doctor. Like most planters he tended himself to the ailments in his household and the quarters.

A shadow fell across the sun. Even Daphne looked frightened. "Your father comes by his terror of illness honestly," she explained. "First he lost your mother, then your sisters. All of the fever."

"Mama died of stomach complaint," Eessa said.

"Don't argue." Daphne sounded bored.

"And Emily and Susan Elizabeth died of the *summer* fever. It comes from the noxious miasmata given off by the swamps at night," Eessa argued.

"Fever is fever," Daddy said, "and it comes from the evil vapors all around this place. And God knows, we have enough of them." He sat down wearily and put his face in his hands. Daphne gave him some cake and champagne. He gulped the champagne.

Sometimes I think my father was haunted by demons and terrors he never mentioned to us: my mother's death and that of my sisters, and his running battle with Grandmother's no-count third husband who had gained control of her money. I know he worried the fact that negroes outnumbered whites on St. Helena's Island. I know it besetted him that he could never please Grandmother, that his older brother Jemmy was the family hero.

Jemmy gazed down at us from an expensive oil portrait even as we spoke.

I took Daddy's silly blue pills. How silly they were, I did not know. Or how good. But they were his mainstay, his magic talisman against sickness. They were like the negroes' blue doors, good for keeping away hants.

"If you don't take them too, Eessa," Daphne said, "I'll not allow John and his parents through the door this day."

Eessa took them. John was her intended. He was the son of Mr. Webb of Ingraham and Webb, the men who sold Daddy's cotton. Eessa May knew she'd pleased everybody by her choice. She also was smart enough to know that she needed Daphne's backing for the elaborate wedding she was planning in the spring. Daddy said it was costing him the gross receipts from twenty bales of cotton.

I got up and walked across the room to Daddy. "We've got to give the shoes, cloth, and rum to the negroes," I said.

That brought him around. We went out back where the goods were piled on the portico. The negroes were already gathered, waiting. Usually

Ty and Garland helped with this chore on Christmas. They had to learn, Daddy said, how to handle servants.

Afterward, the house got quiet, while we waited for the doctor. I wandered, read, ate sweets. When he came, I went to the barn to visit Melody and her eleven pups. On the way back I saw a boat passing in the creek. It had several people on it. An outing.

I watched it glide by, wishing I could be on it. This was not a happy house. I knew Daddy had money trouble. Cotton prices were lower than ever. And you had to be either blind or an idiot not to see that the fences were rotting, the negro houses were becoming mildewed, and the roof of our house leaked.

Daphne entertained beyond their means. She bought things they couldn't afford. And Daddy let her. Or else she complained, nagged, fought with the negroes, criticized his mother.

I felt a hand on my shoulder. Daddy.

"How are the boys?" I asked.

"Dr. Fripp says it's a touch of pneumonia. He's put ointment on their chests and gave them laudanum. They're sleeping."

"Will they be all right?"

"He seems to think so. What are you doing out here in the cold?"

"Watching the steamboat. I wish I could go somewhere."

"You are. I'm taking you to my mother's in

Beaufort tomorrow. I've told Lavinia to pack your things. I'm leaving you there for the two-week school holiday. You'll catch the fever if you stay in this house."

"What about Eessa?"

"She'll stay with the Webbs for a while." There was no arguing the point with him. His mind was set. I felt panic and a sense of elation all at the same time. Two weeks with Grandmother Abigail could be either disastrous or sport, depending on if Lillienfield was around.

"Will Lillienfield be there?" I asked.

"No. He's gone to his place in Charleston to see to some imports."

I despised the man. It wasn't only that he had control of Grandmother's money, it was that their marriage represented a weakness in her. And she was the only strong one in the family. Yet, in some fit of passion, she'd had a marriage contract drawn up a week before she married Lillienfield, saying the profits from her plantations were to be turned over to her husband.

That was five years ago.

Lillienfield was fifteen years younger than Grandmother and three days after they married he found out that she was responsible for all her sons' debts and was using his profits to pay for them.

Right off he mortgaged one of her plantations and ninety negroes. Then he couldn't pay the debt.

That set Daddy and his brother against Lillienfield and put Grandmother in between.

Grandmother did not like being in between. In three months she "withdrew from her husband's society," and went to live in Beaufort on the mainland. And the war was on.

She and Lillienfield were always in Beaufort District Court. Daddy was always contesting, filing bills. Once Lillienfield kidnapped some of our negroes and had to send them back. Another time Daddy pirated some of his provisions right from the wharf in Beaufort.

Uncle Sumner kept out of it, but Grandmother and Daddy were always plotting against Lillienfield. I think they enjoyed it.

"If Lillienfield comes when I'm there, I can't account for what I say to him," I told Daddy.

He put his arm around me. "You must hold your tongue."

"I hate him. He's keeping us poor. He refuses to let Grandmother use her money for anything but his pleasure."

He patted my shoulder. "You know my mother helps out, with gifts and loans so I won't give out."

Daddy lived in fear of "giving out."

Grandmother did send gifts, ducks, bacon, lard. It was her way of outwitting Lillienfield. Once she sent eleven field hands to help dig Daddy's sweet potato slips. Another time she sent a trunk of silk dresses for me and Eessa May. But Daphne gave them to Lillienfield, because he had an emporium in Charleston.

And because he supplied her with opium. Daphne exchanged many of Grandmother's gifts with him for opium. Even while she pretended to hate the man for Daddy's sake.

"Be my good girl and you'll enjoy Mother," Daddy said. "We'll go together. I'll stay and visit a while."

So he had another reason for my visit, then.

The first of the year was bearing down, and Grandmother Abigail would require an accounting from him. Anything he had to tell her would not be good. And I was her favorite.

The next morning I woke early to two sounds. The wind again. And Ty, crying. I sat up in bed.

He was in the doorway of my room. He was dressed and his face was red. I became frightened, thinking he was delirious with fever.

"Daphne," he blubbered. "She's drowning the pups."

I was out of bed like a shot. I put on my robe and followed him downstairs, through the silent, cold house, for not even the house servants were stirring yet.

Out the back door, across the portico and the yard to the barn we ran, Ty sobbing all the time. The wind was biting cold.

Sure enough, just inside the barn door, Daphne knelt on some straw. A bucket of water was in front of her. Her hands were in it, holding something.

I saw bubbles on top. And in the bottom of the bucket one of Melody's pups, held down, helpless.

Another one, already dead, lay on the straw. All the others were squirming around Daphne. And Melody was standing there barking, a high-pitched, distressed sound.

"Stop her!" Ty screamed.

I pushed Daphne aside. She tumbled and landed on the ground. Then I reached into the bucket and pulled out the pup. It was finished.

"How *dare* you!" Daphne pulled herself up to a sitting position. "How dare you accost me like that?"

"How dare you drown these pups?"

"You hurt me. I'm bruised." She got to her feet, rubbing her shoulder.

I could see by the look in her eyes that she was going down-dale from the opium. This was the bad time for her. The tide was going out, leaving the mudflat of her soul exposed.

And that's when I broke the code of silence we had in the house about her filthy habit.

That's when I said the words that got me into trouble.

"You're so taken with opium you don't even know what you're doing!" I shouted. "Your filthy habit is destroying this family!"

She slapped me then. My face stung. I could feel the blood rushing to where her hand had hit. I reeled, then straightened.

"I hate you!" I yelled.

"Your father will hear of this!"

"I don't care! Come on, Ty, grab the pups!"

My brother gathered pups in his arms, three of them. I picked up the bottom of my robe and cradled six. Two were dead.

Daphne had picked up her cane and was about to strike us with it.

Melody stood in front of her, warding her off.

"Run!" I told Ty. And we ran to the house. The wind whipped all around us. The blowing sand stung my face. Melody followed.

We ran up the path from the barn to the house. Daphne couldn't keep up with us. I turned.

She stood there on the wind-whipped ground. Behind the barn and workhouses loomed the forest of oaks, crooked pines, twisted cedars, and palmettos.

The palmetto leaves rattled like skeleton bones in the wind. The myrtle, holly, and prickly pear rustled nervously.

At night the sounds are ominous enough to make me believe what the negroes say, that the Yamassee Indians have come back, to retaliate for the way the negroes, armed by their masters, defended the colony and vanquished the Yamassee and Creek Indians in the Yamassee War of 1715.

"I'll see that your father sends you away from here for good, Amanda, if it's the last thing I do!" Her hair had come unpinned in the wind. She raised her cane to the heavens like some fearful apparition.

Our house is two-story, made of clapboard and perched on a high tabby foundation that's made of sand, lime, oyster shells, and water. There was a hole in the foundation and the boys had made a hiding place underneath.

Ty led the way and I followed. It was dry and warm down in the hiding place. They had some old blankets. And we settled Melody and the pups.

"I'll bring her some food and water," Ty said. His voice trembled.

I felt his forehead. He was burning up. "I'll do it," I said. "You'd best get right back to bed."

Chapter Three

"Your cotton yield for this past year was a third under average," Grandmother said.

"I know, Mother," Daddy answered.

"You had three bales of stained Sea Isle cotton to every fourteen of white."

"Yes." Daddy never disagreed with her.

"Stained Sea Isle cotton brings a fraction of the price of white," she reminded him.

"Rain during the picking season," he said.

"Likely your own bad management is to blame. You don't stay around enough to see your orders carried out."

"Rob Roy carries out my orders."

"Still, you can't run a plantation from a racing skiff. Or a billiards table here in Beaufort. Your daddy always said a planter's footsteps are manure to his land."

Never mind that Grandmother had problems running her own plantations. She never refrained from bringing Daddy to account. As soon as we settled down with our Viennese coffee in her solarium, she started on him.

Sometimes I think my daddy is weak. Oh, he's strong with the negroes; he upholds his honor in the community. But he lets all the women in his life hold sway over him. I don't know why. It grieves me to think on it, so I don't.

I love him so much. I think my love for him and his for me will fix everything, I suppose.

Anyway, there is Grandmother going at Daddy. And him sitting there and sipping his coffee, acting for all the world as if he was at the monthly banquet of his agricultural society.

All the while Grandmother is at her workbench, sculpting clay into a bird right in front of our eyes. Her aristocratic hands never stopped. And she spoke softly, so you never knew she was scolding. Her white hair was piled in curls on top of her head. Her blue eyes sparkled. She wore a loose garment of raw silk over her dress.

"Yamassee is doing fine," Daddy told her.

She smiled. "Yamassee is not doing fine, Ben. You need cash. And you need it fast, if you're to survive. And unfortunately, I am not in a position at the moment to give it to you." She sighed. "You Sea Islanders always did have a way of deceiving yourselves. Did I ever tell you about the time, during the war, when Sea Islanders thought Napoleon was coming? Because they heard he was being exiled to St. Helena's Island?"

"You told me," Daddy said.

Grandmother turned to me. "It was 1815. Old Mr. Capers was selected to greet Napoleon. The whole island made preparations for his arrival. But of course, Napoleon never came. The St. Helena's Island he did go to is in the South Atlantic Ocean, a thousand miles off the western coast of Africa."

I smiled politely. It was a good story. But why did I feel there was some undercurrent pulling between them, which they could not acknowledge in my presence?

"You do deceive yourselves," Grandmother said again. "And you're deceiving yourself, Ben, if you think Yamassee, or your family, can survive without an immediate influx of money. You are planning on sending the boys to Richland, I hope."

Daddy winced. "I'd like to. Garland is interested in the military, Ty in engineering and geology. But the cost is two-hundred-and-fifty dollars each for the year. I can't afford it."

"You must afford it. You went."

All this surprised me. "Are you taking the boys out of the village school, Daddy?" I asked.

He nodded. "They need to be better prepared for life."

What he meant was, they needed to be trained to run the plantation.

"Will I stay in the village school?"

He did not answer. But I saw a look pass between him and Grandmother. And I knew I'd been right about the undercurrent.

— 28 —

They were plotting, I was sure of it. And it had to do with me.

"Why don't you take a walk to my aviary," Grandmother said softly. "I have a new macaw. I know you'll love him."

"I don't want to," I said. "If you're going to talk about me, I want to be here. I'm old enough."

"What makes you think we're going to talk about you, Miss Importance?" Daddy asked.

"Go to the aviary, Amanda," Grandmother said with quiet force. "Yes, we are going to talk about you. You have made problems for your father with this new argument with Daphne. We must decide what to do about it."

There was no shilly-shallying with her when she used that tone. I left the room reluctantly. I took a side door out onto the flagstone path. From there I could look across wide lawns down to the new dock and Beaufort River.

Halfway down the path I looked back. The solarium was glass, so I could see them in there, all cozy. Two calico cats dozed on chairs. Sabrena, Grandmother's favorite servant, was setting a small table with food and lighting candles in the silver candelabra, for it was coming on to dusk. I could see the blue ceiling in the solarium casting its peculiar light. It was the same color as the doors on the negro cabins. Through other windows of the house I saw servants moving around like dusky shadows, polishing, neatening, cooking.

I walked down to the aviary, knowing in my bones that they were deciding my fate.

When I came back half an hour later, Daddy was gone.

Grandmother held her arms out to me. "Come here, we must talk," she said.

And that's when she asked me if I could keep silent for two weeks.

At first I thought she was joking. She always did have what Daphne called "a perverted sense of humor." Daphne said that anybody who would marry a bankrupt pharmacist and allow her sons to find out about the wedding from the newspaper, was possessed of a dark humor.

"Silence, Grandmother?" I stared at her. "You want me not to speak for *two weeks?*"

"Yes."

Sabrena brought in my supper. I stared at the woman, in her bright red turban, as if I'd never seen her before.

"The creamed crab dish is excellent," Grandmother said. "Eat."

I ate. It tasted like sawdust. Especially when she told me how I talked too much, and explained how her request was a challenge, and the time had come to see if I had any character.

Then, when she finished with all that, she asked brightly, "Do you know what else keeping silence does for you?"

"No."

"It makes others confused. Everyone around you gets very confused when you do not speak."

"Why do I have to confuse everyone around me?"

"When those around you are confused, you are strong. Don't you want to be strong?"

It was what Daddy would call a loaded question. He'd once said he'd as soon stand fifty feet from the best Kentucky rifleman as have to answer one of his mother's loaded questions.

"Yes," I said.

"Good. You aren't strong enough, Amanda. Your father and I have been discussing it. The way you pushed Daphne down the other day, the way you flung her opium taking into her face. That was wrong, dear."

The creamed crab dish had gone from tasting like sawdust in my mouth to tasting like mud.

"No, don't protest, dear. I know you were trying to save Melody's pups. But if you truly had strength, you wouldn't have had to push Daphne. Or made mention of the opium."

"What would I have done?"

"Eat, don't let your food get cold."

I ate.

"Do you know how I got strong enough to elope with your Grandfather Nate against my father's wishes?"

"You loved him."

"Love had nothing to do with it. Love can make us weak, silly in the head, cloud our thoughts. Our enemies make us strong. My father was my enemy. My father caused me to recognize strengths I never knew I had when he locked me in my room those weeks. Those long hours in my room made me look inside myself. It's a place most people never go."

She had eloped with Grandfather Nate when she was just fifteen, one year older than I was. They married on the quarterdeck of his ship, the *Swamp Fox*. Her brother Lawrence and her sister, Hannah, had helped her escape her father's house by climbing out the widow walk. On their first voyage, the *Swamp Fox* was destroyed in a hurricane. But they and near all their crew and Cornwallis, their parrot, survived.

She'd never gone back to Salem or seen her father again. Although her sister Hannah had come once or twice to visit, and a niece of hers named Ebie had come, too. That was before I was born.

I wondered if I could leave home and never see Daddy again. I decided I couldn't.

"And then," she was saying, "a few years ago when my second husband, the minister, died, I remembered how I'd gotten that strength through silence and contemplation. So I went, with a Catholic friend from Baltimore, to stay with some nuns for a while. Again, it made me strong."

But not strong enough to keep you from marrying your third husband, I thought.

"Now, Amanda, hear what I say. When one remains silent, all others seek you out. They think you have some secret and wish to know what it is. People cannot stand silence. They fear it like an abyss they may fall into. They fill in that hole with talk. They will tell you *anything*, to fill in that hole. So you not only become strong, you learn the secrets of others."

I asked her then the only logical question I could. "Grandmother, why do I have to get so strong and learn the secrets of others?"

She smiled at me in that maddening way she had. "So you can help me. And your father," she said.

"How?"

But she only shook her head and wagged her finger at me. Then put her finger in front of her lips.

I nodded. But I wondered if everyone in our family didn't have a streak of madness in them.

She reached across the small table and took my hand in her own. "I see so much of myself in you. I succumbed to my weakness and vanity when I married Lillienfield. And look what happened. He lives in Charleston, I live here. And I'm locked in legal battles with him into the next decade. *You must learn to be strong, Amanda, please.*"

Then she produced some paper and one of those newfangled pencils. "Just write down everything you want to say to me."

I took the paper and wrote. "If I do it, will you promise that Daphne won't drown any more of Melody's pups?"

She smiled. "Yes," she said. "I'll speak to your father about it."

And so I stayed silent for two weeks. It was worth doing, to save Melody's pups.

Grandmother allowed me to do just about anything else I wanted on her plantation. It was called Indian Hill and it had limitless possibilities.

Nobody bothered me, the way they did at home. And I didn't have to put up with Eessa May and hear all her stupid talk about her wedding, either.

Grandmother didn't care if I slept late, so I did. She didn't care what I ate as long as I ate. She allowed me to wander the grounds and the woods, to ride any horse in her stables, and to ride astride, not sidesaddle, like I had to do at home.

I visited the barn, watched the servants plant onion sets and Dutch turnips. I made sugar cookies. I stayed up late and read by candlelight. She allowed me to visit with the servants in the quarters if I wished. I was not allowed to do that at home.

I particularly liked visiting Sabrena. She told ghost stories and tales about Br'er Possum, Br'er Rabbit, and Old Sis Fox.

And so I did not speak. Instead, I listened. And I listened well.

I heard the tide, the talk of the negroes in the

kitchen, the banging of pots and pans, the quiet hissing of the fire in the hearth, the blowing of the wind at night, the rattling of some window-panes. I heard the negro songs from the gin house where they were cleaning and packing cotton for market. I heard the soft stomping of the packer forming the cotton in bales with his feet.

I heard Grandmother's shoes on the heartpine floors as she made her rounds, closing the house up for the night. Then the night sounds of a plan-tation at rest, the soft laughter of the negroes, the barking of grandmother's dogs, the baaing of the sheep, the neigh of a horse in the pasture.

I noted the special way voices sound on the water when men took Grandmother's cotton to Charleston on a flatboat.

I enjoyed the choir music in church, because I did not have to join in. I went with Grandmother to her quilting society and heard them fussing with one another over whether to admit women from the island.

They all sounded so shrill. And then, because I did not speak, I became as one invisible. Mrs. Sandiford told a woman, in my presence, how her first husband had taken his own life.

Mrs. Jenkins spoke through me to tell Mrs. Fripp the real reason Reverend McElheran was resigning as pastor of our church. Because twelve-year-old Lucy Pickens had accused him of putting his hands on her when she delivered a pie to the rectory.

I gasped. *Grandmother is right,* I thought. People say things to you and in front of you when you keep silent.

In the kitchen the servants spoke in front of me as if I were not there. I heard Sabrena tell Brister that Lillienfield was coming for a visit and "tonight there be a full moon and you know how it makes him mean, so it's safer all round if'n you get out of sight. Why, the man is so ornery he'll have you flogged if'n you don't take off your hat when you sees him. And he hates you most, Brister."

The first two days afflicted me. I kept trying to speak, then stopped myself. Sometimes Grandmother's look stopped me. Then I'd mind how silly what I was about to say seemed, once I studied on it.

But the real affliction was when Lillienfield came.

He and Grandmother argued. It seemed to go on for hours. Their voices twisted my innards, bruised my bones, making me frightened. His was so loud, I trembled as I listened outside their bedroom, in the hallway. Once I was ready to break my silence and rush in and push the man from the house.

Sabrena stopped me.

Then he left and I heard Grandmother crying softly in her room.

By the end of the first week I was comfortable

in my silence. By the end of the second week I felt a strange lightness, as if I could float in and out of a room and people would regard me as some sort of a spirit.

I felt downright superior and I could have gone on for three more weeks, but Grandmother kissed me and told me it was enough.

"You have the mettle to do what I require," she said.

But she did not tell me, right off, what she required.

"Where did you learn to read cards, Abigail?" Mrs. Fox asked. "Barbados?"

Grandmother smiled and directed Sabrena to set down the tray of coffee and cake. "Ask Brister to stand in the hall and play his violin," she said. Then to Mrs. Fox: "Tarot cards have medieval origins. I learned to read them when I traveled with my first husband."

"Well," Mrs. Pickens said, "I'd like you to tell me if my husband's uncle will leave Charles his estate."

"I'd like to know if I should send my children away to school," Mrs. Boller said.

"And you, Florence?" Grandmother asked.

"I'd like you to tell me if I should take J. Crosby's Compound Bitters for my irregular circulation."

Grandmother sighed. "I think I shall read for Amanda."

The ladies gasped. "She's just a child," Mrs. Pickens said.

"Don't children have more future than any of us?" Grandmother asked. Just then the soulful sound of Brister's fiddle crept through the shadows of the house.

Mrs. Pickens was nettled. "If you know so much of the future, Abigail, how is it you can't avoid your difficulties with Lillienfield?"

Grandmother spread out her cards. "Don't be snide, Amelia, or I won't read for you at all."

Mrs. Pickens pouted, but kept a still tongue in her head.

I shall never forget how Grandmother read the tarot cards for me that night, while Brister played his fiddle in the dark hallway, and Grandmother's macaw, whom she'd named Wellington, sat on her shoulder. She was training Wellington to stay in the house with her now.

She told me I would be going on a long journey, that there would be much sadness on this journey, but much personal gain, also. And that I would become strong.

"Where will I go?" I asked her when she finished. "And who will go with me?"

"You will go by yourself," she said. "You will leave your father and your home, even as I did as a young girl."

I had never before seen Grandmother like this. She spoke from some wellspring of strength and certainty. This was not the same woman I'd heard crying softly in her room, after Lillienfield's visit.

"I could never leave home and Daddy," I said. "Perhaps I'm going *with* Daddy. I'll ask him when he comes to fetch me home tomorrow."

Grandmother gathered up her cards. "Yes, do that," she said.

The candles on the table flickered then, as if the door of the solarium had just been opened to let in the breeze from the water. But there was no open door.

"Read the cards for me now," Mrs. Pickins begged. "My husband's uncle is on his deathbed. I must know if he will leave Charles his estate."

There is something in the very climate of St. Helena's Island that makes us all different. Perhaps it is because the negroes outnumber the whites and we are so acquainted with their superstitions.

Perhaps we are different because we eat too much hominy and bacon. Or is it the lowcountry air? A person can be in the bloom of health one day and dying of some putrid fever the next.

Too much or too little rain can wipe a planter out. So can a late spring frost. A war in some far-off land can drive cotton prices up or down.

People who live like this have to be different. So I tell myself for comfort. So that I won't believe there is some degree of mental derangement in our family. Although Grandmother lives on the mainland, she still suffers from the differences.

That night I heard two hooty owls outside my window, calling to each other. Brister and Sabrena say this in itself is a bad omen. The moon was in its third quarter. It seemed to me that, in between the sounds of the rising tide, I heard Brister playing his lonely fiddle far into the night, down at the quarters.

The next morning Daddy came to fetch me home. Rob Roy came with him.

"How are the boys?" I asked him.

He seemed distracted. They were better, he said. He said nothing else. Through the window I could see Rob Roy setting down some baggage on the portico. I recognized my flowered portmanteau. Then I saw Brister polishing Grandmother's fancy black carriage.

"We *are* going on a trip, Daddy. Why didn't you tell me?" I felt a thrill of excitement. Grandmother's coach was brought out only when we went to Beaufort. The horses' harnesses were studded with silver.

But Daddy could not meet my eyes. "I'll see if Mother needs help," was all he would say. And he got up and went through the hall and out the back door.

I followed.

I caught him just as he was preparing to get into his own carriage.

He was sneaking away from me. And I was seized by panic.

"Daddy!" I ran after him and grabbed his arm. "Why are you leaving me?"

"I told you this was not the way to do it, Ben." Grandmother stepped off the portico. "But you never did listen to me."

"Do what?" I screamed at them.

"I told you to be a man and tell her yourself," Grandmother said.

"Tell me what!" I grabbed Daddy around the waist. "Why are you leaving me?" I demanded.

He took me away from the commotion around the portico, servants staring, dogs mulling about, Grandmother giving orders. He walked across the lawns with me down toward the water. Just short of the dock, he stopped and put his arms around me.

"Forgive me, Amanda. I thought sneaking off was the easy way. But there is no easy way. Mother is right. I must tell you to your face."

"Tell me what? Daddy?"

"We are sending you on a trip."

"Where?"

"North."

The wind was coming off the water, cold. I felt it wrapping itself around my heart.

"North? To school?" I couldn't believe it.

"No, to your grandmother's family, Amanda. In Massachusetts."

I heard someone laugh. In the next moment I

realized it was me. I stared up at him, trying to seek refuge in the familiar contours of his face. "Massachusetts?"

"Yes. Your grandmother needs a better price for her cotton, Amanda. So do I."

My mouth fell open. "What has that to do with me?"

"Everything. We need a new market. Prices in Savannah and Charleston have dropped. Ingraham and Webb said our crops will bring a better price in New England mills. They don't usually use Sea Isle cotton but your great-grandfather has agreed to try it. But only if your grandmother sends one of you up for a visit."

"My *great-grandfather?*"

"Yes. He owns a mill in Lowell. He is very old and would like to see one of his great-grandchildren. Your grandmother thought you would be the one to make the trip."

I pulled away from him, angrily. "Why wasn't I told of this before now?"

He shrugged. "She didn't know before this visit if you could do it. Something you did this visit pleased her."

"Keeping silent," I murmured to myself. "So that was why she made me do it."

"What?" Daddy asked.

I felt anger rising in me, like the tides. "What about Eessa May? Why not send her? She's the oldest."

"She's to be married in the spring, Amanda.

The boys are too young and need their schooling. There is only you."

"Well, I won't go. You can't make me."

"You will go, Amanda," he said sadly. "You must."

"Why must I?" I was crying. I wiped my face with my sleeve.

"Because," he said sadly, "I am very much in debt. And Lillienfield has control of your grand-mother's money and property. Because if we don't get a better price for our cotton, we will give out."

I sobbed quietly.

"The boys must be educated, Amanda," he said quietly. "I must give Eessa May a wedding. The fences need repairing. The roof on the house leaks. Please."

He reached out his hand to me. I ran down the lawn to the edge of the water and stood looking at him.

"Amanda, come out of there. You'll get your feet wet and take a chill."

I stood firm, glaring at him.

"Your grandmother will talk to you. You'll see the sense of it. Come. Say goodbye to me."

But I did not move from my spot.

"Very well, I'll leave then. Since it seems to be the only way to keep you from catching your death."

Then he started to walk back up the slope to the house.

Anger boiled inside me. I felt betrayed. I stood

rooted, watching him go, a sad, slump-shouldered figure, all dressed in black, framed against the gray winter sky.

"My great-grandfather!" I screamed at him. "I never even knew I had one!"

The wind tore the words from my mouth. And in a moment he disappeared from sight.

Chapter Four

"It's a shame you threw your clothes all over," Grandmother said. "Now you'll just have to pick them up. I'll not allow Sabrena to do it."

She stood in the doorway of my room, tall and erect. Her voice was very calm.

Father was gone. Coming to my room, I'd found my portmanteaus. All my clothes from home packed. Likely by Daphne. Well, she'd threatened to have me sent away. How much had *she* had to do with this?

In a fit of rage I'd emptied the portmanteaus all over the floor. Then I kicked them. My breath was spent, my hair in disarray, my throat sore from screaming, and my face red and tear-streaked by the time Grandmother came to see what the commotion was.

"I'm not going!"

She said nothing.

"You plotted behind my back! The two of you! Or was it three? Was Daphne in on this, too?"

"That is beneath you, Amanda."

"You sneaked behind my back and made arrangements. Then you pretended to be my friend. Keep *silent*, Amanda. Everyone around you gets confused when you don't speak. *I'm* the only one confused. Is that what you wanted?"

She sighed. "Spend your emotions and be done with it. We don't have much time. There are things I must say to you."

"*Say* to me? I never even knew *my* great-grandfather was still alive! Now I'm to go and see him? *I hate you! And Daddy!*"

She smiled, sat down, and got a faraway look in her eye. "Do you know how many times I said that to my father? Good. It means you are ready to leave us, then. You see? You are already stronger than when you came to me."

"I am not going!"

"Why stay, when you hate us so?"

I stopped crying. If she was going to use logic on me, I had to have my senses. I hiccuped and rubbed my eyes. I blew my nose into my apron. It gave me time to think.

"I don't have to talk to you. Or him, if I stay here. You taught me that," I said finally.

"But you would forget, in time. You would fall back into our ways. And I want more for you than our ways. They are not good, Amanda. Which is why I want you to leave."

"You want me to leave to get more money for your next cotton crop. Daddy told me. It's a trick.

You're full of tricks, you and Daddy. I don't trust you."

"Good!" she said vehemently. "Don't trust us, ever. You are right. We are full of tricks. We are also shallow and vain. For all the beauty we have here, for all our friends and possessions, the pretense of our elegant ways, we are a people taken with pride, with lethargy, with laziness, and violence. We live off the labor of others. We suck the lifeblood from our negroes, like mosquitoes."

There was a peculiar light in her eyes. And her voice sounded like it did when she was reading her tarot cards.

"You have negroes, hundreds of them."

"It's too late for me to change, Amanda. It isn't for you."

"Why should I change? This is the way I've been brought up."

"I am sending you North. I want you to see what life is like in a place where you don't own others. I want you to pull your own weight. Let your thoughts bloom. And learn independence. You won't learn it here."

"Grandmother."

"No more, Amanda. My two sons are failures. They can't exist without my help. It's our system of slavery. It destroys whites as well as negroes. Do you know that your father will not attend the weddings of any of his negroes? Says the ceremonies are tomfoolery. Yet he fishes with them, he hunts with them, talks with them every day."

I said nothing.

"Do you know that when negro children are born on Yamassee, he registers their names the way he does *colts*? And he will not register the names of the children's sires, though he knows them? Yet he puts down the names of the horses' sires."

"Grandmother, it's his way."

"It's inhuman. And I do not want you growing up thinking it is acceptable."

"Why don't you concern yourself with how Eessa May grows up? Or my brothers? They will take over the plantation someday."

She waved the thought away with her hand. "Eessa May is vain and conceited. Your brothers will be taught to avoid doing any work and to keep power over the negroes. I want you out of that house. Daphne exists on opium. Your father drinks. You are becoming confused. I must deliver you out of the confusion and gloom of your household. And mine."

I felt everything slipping away from me. An undertow of forces I could not understand was making me lose ground. And then I had a thought. "I like it here with you, Grandmother. Why can't I stay here and learn from you? And your mistakes?"

"Because the laws of South Carolina are not kind to women, Amanda. In England the husband's supremacy has been rudely shaken by recent laws. In the North some states are tampering with it. But here in South Carolina, the doctrine of a married woman's subjection flourishes in all its pristine vigor."

She smiled at me. "I want you to at least become acquainted with a place where they are beginning to adopt the independency of married women."

"I'm not marrying yet, Grandmother."

"Your sister is marrying at seventeen. She's lost. Spoiled. So are the boys, already. I am determined to save one of my grandchildren. We start to-morrow. Three days to Charleston in my carriage. By then my cotton should have arrived there, to be put on the same ship we'll take to Baltimore. The Ingrahams will accompany us. I shall visit with my friend in Baltimore. You go on from there with the Ingrahams."

"You're not coming all the way with me?"

"How will you become independent? No. The Ingrahams will be good traveling companions. You may write to me, Amanda."

"Will I come home again?"

"Dear child! Of course. When you are ready."

"When will that be?"

"I will be able to tell from your letters. I will let you know."

Chapter Five

January 1841

Mrs. Ingraham sipped the cream off the top of her coffee. "Did you know," she asked me, "that this is the same hotel where your grandmother asked Mr. Lillienfield to come and meet her right before they were married?"

"No, I didn't." I had never liked Mrs. Ingraham or her husband. They were always trying to find out everyone's private business. They were busybodies. I disliked them even more because I had to travel with them.

Me and one-hundred-and-fifty bales of Grandmother's cotton. On which they were making four percent commission for selling it to Grandmother's own father. I didn't think they deserved the commission. After all, her father wouldn't have accepted the cotton unless I came along with it.

The cotton had arrived yesterday at a Charleston wharf. Mr. Ingraham was having it transferred to the boat we would take to Baltimore. From Baltimore we would take a riverboat up the Chesapeake, stop at Philadelphia where we'd take a coach through New Jersey, then more riverboats.

I liked riverboats about as much as I liked Mrs. Ingraham. Daddy said they were owned by men who often raced them, full of passengers. And that they often sank, or their boilers burst, or they caught fire and burned.

I did not like very much of anything this morning. The world had betrayed me. I saw it as a bad place.

"Please, don't discuss my marriage, Elvira," Grandmother admonished her friend.

"Oh, but it was so *romantic*, the way he met you here and you ran off to marry without telling anyone!"

"It was not romantic," Grandmother said. "It was foolhardy. And I do not wish to have my indiscretions touted as romantic to my granddaughter. How do you feel this morning, Amanda?"

"Better, Grandmother."

When we'd arrived last evening my head had been pounding. Sabrena had given me a headache powder. This morning I woke confused, not knowing where I was. For three nights now it had been a different inn, a different bed, a different room. Yet every morning I woke expecting Eessa May to come bouncing in to borrow a lace collar, or to hear Daphne ordering the servants about. I actually listened for the voices of my brothers below stairs, for the baying of my father's dogs.

Tears had rolled down my face at the thought

of being so far from home. Worse yet, I hadn't been allowed to say a proper goodbye to my brothers or to Rob Roy. What would they say when told I was gone?

"Get up, lazybones," Grandmother had said. She was sitting across the room. Sabrena was doing up her hair. "Put on the new blue dress I bought you. We must go to breakfast."

In the dining room the waiter hovered over her, inquiring after her family. Then he turned to me, offering fish in cream sauce, succulent honey-dipped ham, eggs, fresh fruits and breads and jellies. As if such things could ease my pain.

"Eat," Grandmother said. "You'll feel better."

I ate, and oddly, I did feel better. Which made me feel worse. Was I so shallow then, that the lovely dining room with its rose and white wallpaper, its crystal chandeliers, its Spode china and fresh flowers on the table, could restore my spirits?

"Will you be going to visit the Druggist and Soda Water Establishment this morning, Abigail?" Mrs. Ingraham asked.

That was Lillienfield's drug emporium. Mrs. Ingraham had pointed it out to me last night, on the corner of East Bay and Broad streets.

"No," Grandmother said.

"Do you mind if I go? It's the only place for miles that carries J. Crosby's Compound Bitters."

"Go, Elvira," Grandmother said, "but tell Mr. Lillienfield that if he comes to this hotel, I will not receive him."

Grandmother smiled at me when Mrs. Ingraham left. "I'm glad she's gone. You and I have much to talk about this day."

The only thing I wanted to talk about was home. I hated the world outside our hotel window, the strange faces, the unnatural tempo of things. I missed things I never knew were part of me. Like the hooty owl outside my room at night, the sound of the breeze in the sea grasses, the comforting sight of the blue doors on the negro houses, the way the palmetto leaves rattled in the wind. I worried about Melody's pups. Would Daddy keep his word? Grandmother said he promised not to let Daphne try to drown them again.

Back in our suite of rooms Grandmother drew something out of one of her trunks. It was an oilskin bag, long and narrow.

From it she drew part of a quilt and laid it out on the bed. "Amanda, this is a piece of the quilt I brought from home when I left as a young girl. My sisters and I were working on it together. We each took a piece. Of course, I've added to mine."

I stared at her, and it. Vaguely I recollected something about a quilt that had been rescued when the *Swamp Fox* went down on that first trip she'd taken with Grandfather Nate.

It was in that part of my mind consigned to family folklore. Like the story of how all the whites on St. Helena's Island started taking guns to bed the year I was born, because there was rumor afloat about a slave uprising. And my father's brother,

Uncle Sumner, discharged his in his sleep and nearly blew his own head off.

The quilt was a bit faded. Her name was embroidered on the bottom: Abigail Chelmsford Videau.

"I've kept it in this bag ever since it survived the wreck," she said.

"It's beautiful, Grandmother. What's the bird in the middle?"

A peculiar-looking bird formed the centerpiece.

She smiled. "That bird was drawn on the back of a letter Grandfather Nate sent me in 1808 from aboard the rebuilt *Swamp Fox*. There was a boom in English cotton manufacturing. At fifty-two cents a pound, your grandfather wanted to take his cotton to England himself."

She got a dreamy look in her eyes. "The English needed our cotton, but at the same time they were stopping our ships and impressing the men on board. Your grandfather came back by way of the Canary Islands to drop off some English goods. A British ship was pursuing him. He was anchored in a cove in the Canaries, sick with fever and eluding them when he wrote me the letter."

She took another oilskin bundle from the same trunk, unwrapped it, and drew forth a Bible. From it she removed a piece of paper. "Here is that letter with the bird drawn on it." She handed it me.

The letter was fragile. Both her name and Grandfather's were worn off. But there was some writing.

*Here at the Canaries ten days . . . we're all sick
. . . can't fight the British . . . hiding . . . victuals
enough for one more week . . . steward rowed ashore
for water . . . I saw this bird yesterday. . . beautiful
. . . gave me hope . . . know how you love birds
. . . miss you . . . next mailing from De Janeiro
. . . long voyage . . .*

And there was the sketch of the bird on the back.

"His health was never the same after that voyage," Grandmother said. "He died four years later. I put the bird in the center of my quilt. You see, my sisters and I agreed that every patch in the quilt should be designs and fabrics only from those we loved and trusted."

I nodded.

"This bit of fabric is from the jacket of Captain Barr of the *Suffolk*, the ship that picked us up in the storm. These two squares are from friends of his who opened their home to us in the Canary Islands after the wreck."

I listened, knowing this was important to Grandmother. But more than that — it was from her past, something she seldom spoke of except for references to Grandfather Nate.

Her past was my past.

She was telling me about myself.

"This is a patch from Liddy's dress. She and her husband, Merlin, were your grandfather's servants. He treated them well."

"And this?" I asked.

"A piece of Jemmy's uniform coat from when he was hit on the *Constitution*." She folded the quilt and put it and the Bible back in their oilskin bags. "You may have them both. Keep both wrapped in oilskin and close to you. Especially on the steamboats. Keep the letter in the Bible. Always."

I looked at her in astonishment.

"You must take the quilt home. To my people in Lowell."

"Why?"

"It's time I sent it home. And you with it."

I was taken aback. And then a thought took hold of me, chilling my bones. "Are you sickly, Grandmother?" I was frightened.

"Sickly?" She laughed. "Me? I may be an old lady indulging in her whims, but I'm as strong as an ox."

"People do these kinds of things when they're dying."

She put her arms around me. "I'm not dying, dear. I've just decided it's time to do certain things, that's all. My part of the quilt should be pieced together with the rest of it. Who will see to it if I don't? My sister, Hannah, is dead. So is Thankful. And my brothers, Cabot and Lawrence. Cabot's daughter Ebie and her husband run things for the old man. I want you to bring the quilt to her."

"What kind of bird is it?" I asked.

"We never found out. He never saw it but that once. Strange, isn't it?" She laughed. "The only one of my immediate family who is still alive is my father. He's ninety-three. Can you believe it? The good die, Amanda, and the wicked live on."

Chapter Six

I sat on my bed in our hotel room in Baltimore, watching Grandmother sleeping. I was fully dressed, in a warm new coat, hat trimmed with fur, and shiny new boots. I was all ready to leave. The Ingrahams were fetching me to catch the riverboat, which left in an hour.

Grandmother had been up, retching all night.

Between bouts of sleeping, I'd heard her, seen Sabrena's long shadow cast against the wall as she attended her.

"Just stomach," Sabrena had whispered to me. "Something she ate at dinner. Go back to sleep."

But I had long since known that nothing was just anything in the middle of the night. My mother had died of stomach fits. After you lose your mother you may as well forget about nights. They are never good for you again.

In the morning Sabrena roused me, helped me dress, and sent me down to breakfast with the Ingrahams. I'd come back upstairs to find her slumped in a chair across the room, sleeping.

Sabrena snored. It was a lonely sound. My daddy snored, too. And I was frightened. Sickness terrified me. When it came on at home you could be walking around fit as a fiddle one minute and at death's door the next.

I heard the Ingrahams' voices across the hall.

Should I wake Grandmother? Or just leave? We'd said our goodbyes last evening. But it felt wrong, just leaving. Besides, there was something I must ask her.

Then, as I moved on the edge of the bed, my dress rustled and her eyes opened. She smiled.

"Hello."

"How are you feeling?" I asked.

"Better. That Sabrena is a wonder. I don't know what she gave me, but it made everything calm down."

"What's ailing you?"

"Something I ate for dinner."

"We both ate the same fish."

"Yes, darling, but you're not sixty-eight years old."

I thought that poor reasoning, then decided no. She looked old this morning. But how did the fish know it? This one's sixty-eight, I'll make her sick? The other one's only fourteen, there's plenty of time?

"Grandmother, how can I leave you like this?"

"Sabrena is taking me, today, to the nuns."

I stared. She had lied to me. Why was I surprised? She'd done a lot of lying to me of late.

"You said you were going to see your friends here in Baltimore."

"The nuns are my friends."

"You're not even Catholic, Grandmother."

"You don't have to be Catholic for the nuns to let you stay a while and gather yourself in. I need to gather myself in, Amanda."

I hated it when she spoke about gathering herself in, like she was a cotton crop. "Grandmother, there's something I need to ask you," I said.

She struggled to sit up. "And there's something I need to tell you. Help me, dear."

I did so, propping the pillows around her. "Shall I wake Sabrena?"

"No." She took my hand. Hers was hot, mine cool. "You first, go ahead."

"I thought your family lived in Salem. Why are you sending me to Lowell?"

"They moved to Lowell fourteen years ago, when my father chose a new site for his factory. There was good water power there."

"You said your sister Thankful was dead. But I recollect once that you told me she had a daughter. Will I meet her in Lowell?"

She gave me a thin smile. "Likely you will. She was sent back home years ago, after Thankful died. She didn't have an easy time of it. She's half-Indian, you know. The only way they were able to prove she belonged to the family was by *her* piece of the quilt, which Thankful had given her. As I give mine to you. But it got mislaid for a while. Since she couldn't prove who she was, my father had her working in the kitchen, then the last I heard she had some position of importance in his new mill."

"Did she find the quilt to prove who she was then?"

"Yes, eventually. Jemmy met her before that, when he went there just before he was killed. He wrote that she was just lovely. She hadn't been able to prove who she was. But Jemmy always believed she was family. So hold onto your piece of the quilt, Amanda."

I smiled. "I won't need to prove myself, Grandmother. They asked to see me, remember?"

"Hold onto it anyway," she insisted. "And always keep it in oilskin on the boat."

"You're tired. You should sleep."

"I'll have plenty of time for that. Listen. I've been telling you all along that I want you to be strong. It isn't enough, being strong. You must do something with the strength you gain. You must make your mark on the world. You must help others."

This was too serious. I didn't have the mettle for it. "Don't worry, Grandmother, I'll be fine."

"If you just store up strength inside you, it turns to power. And before you know it, you're using it on others. Power is a bad thing to have, Amanda, if you don't help those less fortunate than you. Your father has it over the negroes. All the men in the South do. In the end it weakens those who have it and waters down all their good qualities."

"Grandmother, I'll never have any power. Women don't. You just told me that."

Her grip tightened on my hand. "You will have it someday. I know it. I saw it in my tarot cards."

Not *them* again. But that put me on notice. She seldom spoke of what she saw in her cards. Oh, she'd told me of this trip the night she read for me, but she'd known of it all along.

"Promise me you will help others when you have been given the power," she said.

The look in her eyes frightened me. I promised. But I didn't like any of this. It was too much for me. I felt like picked cotton. Once again I thought there was something wrong with my Grandmother, some streak of dementia coming out in her old age. Then I reminded myself that she had always had this sense of drama. She never did anything in a simple way.

A soft knock sounded on the door.

"Go," she said.

But I could not move. How could I just walk out the door? "Grandmother," I said.

"Go, I can't have Mrs. Ingraham see me like this. She'd tell everyone in Beaufort." And she gave me one of her beatific smiles, the kind that wrung the heart out of me. "You look lovely in that blue dress and cloak, Amanda. Blue is your lucky color. Always remember that. Take comfort in things blue, always."

So I kissed her and, tears blinding my eyes, I went.

It was when we were standing at the window of the purser's office on the riverboat that I first saw the girl.

I think I took note of her because she was wearing blue and Grandmother's words still hung in my mind.

Up until then I hadn't really noticed anything. My heart was numb at leaving Grandmother. I just followed the Ingrahams and their mulatto servant, Florence, through the confusion of the great shed, up the gangway, and onto the quarterdeck.

Mr. Ingraham was arguing with the purser. "This is intolerable. The rooms were reserved!"

"I'm sorry, sir, but we have no record of it!"

"I paid for them!"

"Your room is very large, sir. You could have the little girl stay with you and her mother."

"She is not our child. But we are responsible for transporting her."

"Oh." The purser rattled through some papers and cleared his throat, nervously. "I only have one free room at the moment. It's the grand stateroom. We're under orders always to keep it ready for the president of Old Union Line. I suppose we could let you have it, but it does come dear."

That silenced Mr. Ingraham. Like people who are always talking about making money, spending it usually shut his mouth.

"How about me? We could make room." The girl in blue stepped forward. She was tall and pretty. Brown-eyed, brown-haired. She had a companion, yes, a girl about my age. They had no servant. Her blue traveling suit, on second glance, spoke of "genteel poverty."

"Ah, Mrs. Rhordan, bless you," the purser said.

She smiled. "I and my sister would be happy to welcome so well-bred a young woman into our company for the trip. If her guardians would permit it."

And with that she stuck out a gloved hand. Right at Mr. Ingraham, who, though he knew how to take four percent commission from Grandmother for selling cotton to her own father, did not know what to say to a young girl — traveling without benefit of male companionship — who offered to help him out of a predicament.

Mrs. Ingraham then showed more sense than I had given her credit for. "George, get the receipt for your refund and I will speak to this young woman. Florence, gather my bags."

She led Mrs. Rhordan aside. I was left standing with her sister.

"My name's Clara," she said. "What's yours?"

"Amanda."

Dark, fat curls peeked out from under her bonnet and she was dressed in the same blue as her sister.

"Elinora's gone and stuck her nose in again where it doesn't belong. She's always doing it.

Saving people. Though we ourselves need saving."

I bristled. "Well, she needn't bother. I have money. I can pay for passage in the grand stateroom. My daddy always said, 'What good is money if you don't have pride?' "

She grabbed my arm as I started to move back to the purser's office. "Don't be silly. You Southerners are all alike. You can't eat pride. Elinora and I are glad to have you."

"How do you know I'm Southern?"

She laughed. "Have you listened to yourself speak lately? I'd venture to say it was the Carolinas. Am I right?"

I glared at her. Her own accent was flat and nasal. *A Yankee,* I thought. *Dear God, I've met my first Yankee.* "North or South?" I challenged her.

"South."

"How do you know?"

She shrugged. "I just do. And you're rich, too, probably a planter's daughter."

I peered into her face. It was pale. She seemed anxious. Whatever was making her anxious had taken the bloom of prettiness off her. "Are you clairvoyant? Like my grandmother?"

"No. But you're traveling with a mulatto servant."

"She belongs to the Ingrahams."

"See what I mean? You said *belongs.* Where I come from people don't belong to others."

"Where's that?"

She ignored the question. "And somebody who

talks about her daddy like you do, comes from money. Who has a daddy?"

I saw tears in her eyes. "Don't you have one?"

She gave me a brittle smile. "Don't pay mind to me. I'm the hard one, though I'm younger. Elinora's soft. If she weren't, she wouldn't have gotten herself into this kettle of fish to begin with."

"I don't consider myself a kettle of fish."

"Oh no, not you. We have other concerns. You wouldn't believe it. And I'm not allowed to say."

Just then, Mrs. Ingraham came toward us. "Amanda, Mrs. Rhordan and her sister are going to Lowell! By the same route as we are! Aren't we lucky?"

I wasn't quite sure. I had an uneasy feeling.

"The purser himself knows her. And I have questioned her. She and her sister come from Lowell! Their older sister runs a boardinghouse there for your great-grandfather! They have graciously offered to share their room with you all the way to Philadelphia. It'll be ever so much more pleasant than having to travel with us dull old folks, won't it?"

Ever so much more, I told myself.

"Come along then, George. Come, Florence. We'll go upstairs and find our rooms. We're not even underway yet and I'm all tuckered out."

She seemed happy to be rid of me.

We went through the grand saloon, where people were milling about in confusion. You could hear the thuds on the side of the boat as the cargo was being loaded. All the passengers were scurrying for their rooms.

Mrs. Ingraham hailed a porter. Elinora, Clara, and I struggled with our own portmanteaus. Up the stairs and along the gallery we went, until we found their room. It had two large beds. One was curtained off.

Elinora flushed. "My husband was supposed to accompany us. Business detained him."

Suddenly the whole ship shuddered, a gong went off, and I heard a grinding noise. "Oh." I sank down on my bed.

Elinora smiled for the first time. "Oh, the last bells. Listen." She strode across the room and opened the little window.

"All that ain't goin', please to git ashore." We heard the negro voice, firm and clear over the din.

Then we felt a great lurch, a gong sounded and I heard another grinding noise.

Elinora closed the window. "The paddle wheel has started to turn. Why don't you unpack, Amanda? Clara, help her, she looks white in the face."

I was in terror of the riverboat, of the noises, the steam, the confusion. But as we steamed up the Chesapeake there were sights and sounds to distract me — other passengers to watch, the track of foam from the great wheel, the sight of the officers in the wheelhouse, the ringing of the ship's bell.

In the dining room I watched people who acted as if they were sitting in their own houses, instead of steaming up the bay in the dark with the twinkling lights from shore rushing by. And I wondered if I was the only one so terrified.

Right off, I sensed Elinora was hiding something.

For one thing, she was always looking over her shoulder. For another, she knew a powerful lot about riverboats for a woman who claimed to be just traveling on one. And then she worried inordinately if Clara was out of her sight for more than ten minutes.

I'd been around Grandmother enough to know when someone has something to hide.

In the dining room that first night she took the head waiter aside and asked for a table away from everyone. No sooner were we seated in an obscure corner than she clutched her napkin. "Clara, do you see that man over there in the gray suit?"

"It isn't him," Clara said.

"Are you sure?"

"Don't you think that I know him by now, Elinora?" There was something in Clara's voice that put me on notice. Some manner superior to her older sister. If I talked to Eessa May like that she would have scratched my eyes out.

"Yes, I'm sorry, of course you would know, dear," Elinora said.

Across the room I saw the Ingrahams dining with friends. I smiled, but did not wave. Somehow I minded I must not draw attention to us. I was glad I didn't have to sit with them, glad I didn't have to listen to the latest fluctuation of cotton prices on the world market.

"I recommend the fish, madam," the waiter said. "It's perch. And much fresher than the shoulder of mutton."

Elinora smiled. "Thank you. I think I'll have a glass of wine with my meal."

"Good," Clara agreed, "it will gather you in. You need that now."

It was in that moment that I knew what their problem was.

Elinora had husband trouble. Like Grandmother. That was all folderol, that business she'd told me about her husband not being able to make the trip.

She was hiding from her husband.

I knew all the signs. I'd seen the same actions on Grandmother when she was expecting Lillienfield at her plantation and she hid and bade the servants tell him she was out.

"Well, Amanda," Elinora asked me, as she sipped her wine, "are you still frightened of the riverboat?"

"Who said I was frightened?"

Her laugh was girlish. "You can't hide it."

"I just wonder how the officers can see what's ahead of us in the dark."

"Pilots. They're called pilots. And they know the waters. It's their job. They're very good at it. It's all they really care about. Their pride and prestige are all to them."

There was a deadness in her voice. And I knew then that her husband was a steamboat pilot. And that was why the waiter knew her and gave us the quiet table in the corner and told us that the perch was fresher than the mutton.

Chapter Seven

In the night I woke up frightened. The world was moving under me.

At home, when I woke up frightened to find the world moving under me, there were things I could do about it. Walk around the house, touch familiar things, wander outside. I could go to the kitchen and get some warm milk and honey.

If I wandered outside now, I'd be in the Chesapeake Bay.

I'd been dreaming of Daddy on Black Hawk, only Black Hawk was sick with the distemper and Rob Roy was trying to smoke him up the nostrils. Black Hawk was furious and Daddy was hard put to rein him in. And all around Daddy's feet, ready for the hunt, were Melody's pups instead of his possum hounds.

All the pups, even the ones Daphne had drowned.

I lay listening to the night noises of the riverboat, the rhythm of the paddle wheel, some music from the grand saloon, the sound of the water.

All sounds that were foreign to me. I clutched my reticule with Grandfather Nate's Bible in it. Then came a sound that was not foreign.

Someone was crying.

Ah, here was something familiar. Grandmother cried when Lillienfield visited. Daphne cried when she was too far down-dale from the opium. Eessa May cried when her hair didn't do up right. Here was familiar ground.

I got up and pushed aside the curtain. Moonlight streamed in the window. I could see Clara, sitting on the floor.

She was the one crying.

"Clara?" I whispered. "What's wrong?"

It was cold as the inside of the devil's ear in the room, and I was reminded that it was January, and our boat was cutting its way through the Chesapeake, deeper and deeper into the North. Madness, pure and simple. Nobody who was of sound mind went North in winter. I figured that before all this was finished, the cold alone would probably kill me.

Clara was shivering. I put my arms around her, as I would have around Ty or Garland. "Tell me."

"I'm afraid."

"Of the boat?" She had been so unafraid, mocking me, not in an unkind way, but to make light of my terror.

"The boat? I wish that were all I had to be afraid of."

I felt stupid then, childish. Because she sounded so much older and wiser. To show her I wasn't some silly little noodlehead, I let her know what I had surmised. "You're afraid of Elinora's husband, aren't you?"

That did the trick. She wiped her nose with the sleeve of her flannel nightgown and regarded me with new respect. "How did you know?"

Elinora stirred in her sleep. I motioned to Clara to come with me, behind my curtain. She followed. We sat on my bed. We bundled in the blankets.

I told her about Grandmother and her husband.

She listened, solemnly. "Does he beat her? Like Nicholas beats Elinora?"

"No." I thought at first that she was conjuring up some story to make her sister out larger than life to me. Part of me liked Clara. But part of me knew she was a sly piece, craving attention. She had no father. Likely she would say just about anything to get attention.

"My daddy would shoot him if he did," I told her.

"Nicholas beats Elinora," she whispered. "It's good when he's away on a trip. We have grand times. But that changes when he comes home. Especially if he's been drinking."

I did not know what to say. I wanted her to continue, and I didn't want to hear anymore, all of a piece.

"He pilots the *Kosciusko*. Do you know what people call it? The *Cask-o-whiskey*. His whole crew drinks."

"How can he pilot it?"

"He says he does better when he's in his cups than when he isn't. Likely he does. But when he comes home, he starts in on my sister. Did you see the purple bruise on her left cheek?"

"No."

"She covers it with powder. When she wakes up in the morning, you'll see it. She'll tell you she bumped into a door. But she lies. He hit her last time he was home."

I nodded.

"I came down from Massachusetts to visit her a year and a half ago. It was supposed to be a short visit. I live with my sister Emma, who runs a boardinghouse there. We didn't know he'd been beating Elinora. She never told us. I begged her to run away, to go home with me to Lowell. I wouldn't leave her so I stayed on."

"But you finally convinced her to leave."

"Yes, but not because he was beating her. I don't ever think she would have left for that. She left to keep me safe."

"He hits *you?*"

"No." She looked down at the blanket. She picked the lint off it. "That I could abide."

"What does he do to you?"

She raised her eyes and looked at me. Even in the moonlight I could see a knowledge in those eyes that did not belong there. *Why she's older than fourteen*, I minded. I saw the years stamped there on her face. And I knew then what she meant.

She was tagged, like my father's stained Sea Isle cotton.

Stained, the tag read when he shipped it.

"Oh." I breathed the word almost like a prayer, cursing my own stupidity. "I'm so sorry, Clara."

"So am I. So is Elinora. It's why she's so daft about not letting me out of her sight. So now you know. We've run away."

I'd been right about them, then.

"Only I'm afraid he's following us."

"What makes you think that?"

"He said he would, if we ever left. He said he'd never let her go."

"Does he know you're on your way to Lowell?"

"He knows we come from there, though he's never visited. And never allowed Elinora to go home since they married. They wed four years ago. Elinora was down here visiting friends and she met and married him in three months. Since she never came home afterward, I came to see her."

"Why didn't he let her go home?"

"He says Elinora puts on airs. She talks about people in Lowell who have money. Like your great-grandfather. Is Mr. Chelmsford really your great-grandfather?"

"Yes."

"He's one of the richest people in Massachusetts."

"I don't even know him."

She sighed. "I'm never going to love a man. Never."

She was really shivering now. I made her lie down and covered her and then I lay down next to her on the bed. In a little while she was asleep. I heard her measured breathing.

I lay there in the dark, listening to the sound of the water against the boat, the ship's bells. *So, Grandmother*, I thought, *you wanted me to go North. To see what life is like in a place where people don't own others.*

Well, it seems there are different ways of being owned. Don't you know this? You think all the hatred, all the meanness and cruelty come from the South.

What will things be like when I get further North, I wondered? And on that thought I fell asleep and again I dreamed.

I saw Daddy on Black Hawk again. Melody and her pups were there, too. Only this time all the pups were dead.

The next morning Clara was in good spirits. You would think the night before never happened.

We went to breakfast. From the dining room windows you could watch the sparkling water and the distant shoreline. We were passing a lot of flat farmland. Acres of it. On the shoreline I saw some people watching us, so small they looked like ants. And I thought, there's a girl like me with those people. And she's wishing she could go on a trip somewhere. Little does she know.

At breakfast, Elinora walked over to the Ingrahams' table and spoke with them a while and came back smiling. "They gave permission for you to travel with us the rest of the way," she said.

I looked up from my plate of eggs and fish. "What?"

"Well, you want to, don't you?" she asked. "We'll have great sport. As far as the riverboat goes. All the way to Connecticut."

I said yes, of course. But somehow I could not connect the word "sport" with these girls. I pondered that neither of them even knew the meaning of the word.

So we traveled together. In Philadelphia the Ingrahams, Florence, Clara, and Elinora and I took a four-horse carriage to Trenton. It was a morning's ride. We took our noon meal at an ordinary in Trenton. Then we got back into the coach for an afternoon's ride, over rut-filled icy roads to Princeton.

I don't know which was worse, getting jostled in the carriage or having to hear Mrs. Ingraham talk. She was one of those people Grandmother had told me about, who was afraid of silence. It was a hole she would fall into. For a while Elinora tried to keep up the conversation, then pleaded a headache. Mr. Ingraham slept and snored.

Clara was reading *Pickwick Papers* the whole

time, oblivious of Mrs. Ingraham's chatter. She read an awful lot, I noticed. I was sorry my own books were packed away. Soon Mrs. Ingraham fell asleep, too.

We stayed the night in Princeton at the Mansion House Hotel, next to Joline's Tavern. Again I ate and roomed with my new friends. In the morning, Clara woke me early. We dressed quickly in front of the fire and crept from the room, down through the dining room and foyer and into the street.

I had asked no questions. Clara was up to something and had been kind enough to include me.

I was both honored and ready.

On the street she looked at me. "Breathe that air! What a beautiful morning!"

"It's freezing!" I huddled in my coat.

"Let's walk!"

We looked in shop windows. We bought sweet buns and hot cider from a vendor on the street. She pointed to the Presbyterian church across the street. "When I came through here a year and a half ago on my way to visit Elinora, the old church was set afire by a rocket on the Fourth of July," she said. "It was burning."

I thought her well-traveled. And I minded that something was going on here that was more than just sneaking out for sweet buns and hot cider.

We were becoming fast friends. She told me about her sister, Emma, back in Lowell. "Emma has her feet on the ground. Elinora is flighty."

"And you?"

"I'm the little sister. They each try to exert their influence on me. They're rivals. But when it comes down to it, they have more in common with each other than with me. Because of their age. I feel left out."

"I don't get on with my sister at all," I told her.

She smiled. "I'm learning from both their mistakes, but they don't know it."

"What will you and Elinora do in Lowell?"

"Emma is getting us work in the mill."

"The mill?"

"The Merrimack Manufacturing Company. Your great-grandfather's mill. It's a good place to hide out. And earn wages. We must have work."

"Of course," I said. "How silly of me. Maybe my great-grandfather will allow me to visit you in the boardinghouse."

She laughed. "Not likely. But I'll tell you what. Mill girls have plenty of time to improve themselves. They go to reading rooms and lectures. Maybe we can meet at a lecture on occasion. Would you like that?"

I brightened. "Yes."

We were walking by the main campus of the College of New Jersey. She stopped and pointed. "Any one of those professors walking there to class might be my father," she said.

I became angry. "Don't, Clara. You don't have to."

"Don't what?"

"Don't tell some wild tale to appear important to me. You don't have to do that. You're my friend."

Her eyes filled with tears. "But it's no tale. I wish it were. You know how you don't know your great-grandfather?"

"Yes."

"Well, I don't know my father. He ran away from my mother when I was a baby. We lived in Boston then. Mama could scarcely put bread on the table after he left. She worked as a seamstress. Emma was already married and had a child before I was born."

She laughed. "I'm younger than my niece. Anyway, after my father left we moved to Lowell where Mama got the job running the factory boardinghouse. Emma's husband was a sailor and he was lost at sea. When Mama died, she came to Lowell and took charge of the boardinghouse. And me. I went to school until I was ten. Then I helped Emma in the boardinghouse."

My chest hurt. Tears stung my eyes. "Oh, Clara, I'm sorry."

"It's one reason why Elinora wouldn't leave Nicholas. She had this notion that married people should stay together, no matter what."

"It's all right," I said. "We can't help who our people are."

She grinned. "Fancy you should say that. Come on, let's go back to the hotel for breakfast. I'm starved."

We ran all the way back to the Mansion House. We were the first ones in the dining room. Feeling very important, we ordered a pot of tea and a large order of buckwheat cakes with honey and butter. Clara poured the tea.

"I plan on working at the mill for about four years," she said, "and saving my money. All the mill girls save money. For dowries, to send brothers to college, to help out at home. Do you know what I'm going to do with my money?"

"What?"

"I plan to go to college."

"Girls don't go to college," I said, "they can't."

"Maybe not in the South. But in the North you can."

"Where?"

"Oberlin. In Ohio."

"They take *women?*"

"They even take negroes."

I could not believe it. *Negroes.* I thought of Rob Roy, who could read and figure and track the rows of corn and weigh the cotton and carry out all Daddy's orders. I wondered if Grandmother knew about Oberlin. Here was a place in the North that not only thought of negroes as people, but set out to educate them. I must tell Grandmother.

Then I saw Elinora coming down the stairs. She waved at us and came toward the table.

"Don't tell her I told you about our father," Clara cautioned.

"You don't have to worry," I said, "we're friends."

It wasn't until we boarded the *Bellona* in New Brunswick that evening that I remembered I didn't know the name of the boat that had taken us from Baltimore to Philadelphia.

"*Water Witch*," Elinora told me. "The *Bellona* is owned by Cornelius Vanderbilt. For a long time there were laws against running a steamboat in New York waters. Only certain men could do it. Vanderbilt helped break the monopoly."

Once Elinora got talking about riverboats, she never stopped. She knew all about them.

By dusk we were in Staten Island, where we changed to another riverboat. The *Nautilus*.

Since it was only an hour's ride to Whitehall Slip in Manhattan, we sat in the grand saloon, which wasn't half so grand as it should have been. We were all exhausted when we finally reached Manhattan. And nobody was doing much talking. Not even Mrs. Ingraham.

Darkness had fallen. Snow was starting to come down and I became very excited. I'd never seen snow. But we were soon jostled aboard another steamboat and had to find our rooms.

Supper was being served. I was starving. Mrs. Ingraham had a migraine. Florence was scurrying about, talking to waiters, rustling up food to take to her room.

In the dining room I was in pure delight. Fresh

flowers were on all the tables. Someone played a violin in the far end of the room.

"Oh, it's elegant," I breathed. I looked at Clara. She was very white and still. A few moments before in our cabin, she had been as excited as I. What had happened?

Elinora smiled. "You're becoming a seasoned traveler, Amanda."

"What's the name of this boat?" I asked her.

"The *Lexington.*"

We ordered our supper. Creamed lobster. Clara didn't eat or talk much. She kept biting her lower lip and sliding her eyes out the windows.

"What's wrong?" I whispered.

She nibbled some bread. "Soon as we can, let's go to our room. I'll plead sick."

I agreed. She was up to something. I didn't know what, but it was serious this time. That I did know.

When the time came to order dessert, Elinora looked up at the waiter. "Shouldn't we have been underway by now?"

"There's been a delay, madam. We were waiting for a substitute engineer to come aboard. He arrived about fifteen minutes ago."

"Oh?" Elinora asked. "Is there a problem?"

The man hesitated.

She smiled. "I don't frighten. My husband is a riverboat pilot out of Baltimore. You can tell me."

"Ah, yes, madam." And he leaned down to whisper. "The captain is concerned about the operation of the engine. The boilers have built up excessive heads of steam. The engineer we are waiting for is an expert."

"Of course." Elinora smiled at us reassuringly. "It will be all right, girls. Nothing to worry about."

"Can we go for a turn on the deck?" Clara asked. "We don't really want dessert. I need some air."

"It's chocolate cake," Elinora said.

"Amanda has never seen snow," her sister countered.

"Very well, but get your warm coats on. I'll sit here and enjoy my coffee and cake."

I left with Clara. It wasn't fair that I had to choose between snow and chocolate cake. It was less fair that someone else was doing the choosing for me. Something had happened to my life lately, I decided. It was like a carriage with four runaway horses. I kept feeling that if I could only grab the reins on one of them, I would be all right.

The runaway carriage that symbolized my life was about to take another turn. In the room, Clara took my coat and started putting it on.

"You've got the wrong one," I said.

"Oh, do I?" She laughed and took it off. "I'm sorry, I should have asked you. I need to wear it."

For a moment I did not understand. It isn't as if I don't know danger when I see it. Our house is full of it, inside and out. Outside we have wild-cats, always after the small game and poultry. Inside we have Daphne, after anybody she can get.

"Why do you need my coat?"

"I need more than your coat, Amanda. I need you to change clothes with me. Dress, bonnet, shoes."

"Why? Is this some kind of game?"

"I suppose. In a way. Nicholas is on board. I saw him in the wheelhouse. And when we were going into the dining room I heard a crew member say he was the substitute engineer."

"Are you sure?"

"I'd know Nicholas anywhere."

"I thought he worked out of Baltimore."

"He does. And he doesn't know anything about boilers. He's a pilot. The only thing I can think of is that he saw a way to get aboard by pretending to be someone else."

"Oh." I needed to ask questions, but I didn't even know what they were yet. She did.

"Likely the real substitute engineer is in his cups somewhere and Nicholas paid him off."

I was amazed at her acquaintance with the ways of not only grown-ups, but also of evil. Hearing her speak was like having a curtain part to reveal a whole other person behind the fat silken curls and the demure dress.

"Will you do it?" she asked. "Will you help me?"

"How can our changing clothes help?"

"I need to tell the captain. But I can't have Nicholas recognize me. Do you want the boilers to explode and kill everyone? There are one hundred fifty people on this boat."

I didn't want to hand over my dress and ermine-trimmed coat to Clara. She'd held too much sway over me already. More than that, her determination and self-importance struck me wrong. "Why do *you* have to be the one to tell the captain?"

"Elinora would panic. And there isn't time to explain to anyone else."

I wanted even less to be responsible for one hundred and fifty people being killed. I started to unbutton my dress. I supposed this was what Grandmother meant by helping others.

Within a few minutes we were changed into each other's clothing. "Give me your reticule," Clara said.

I clutched it closer. "No." There were limits, after all.

"You live with that thing. What's in it?"

"My Bible. Clara, do you think there's any real danger with the boilers?"

"If I don't see the captain soon, there will be."

"Then I'm taking something else with me. Wait." I picked up Grandmother's quilt in the oilskin bag at the end of my bed. The story of how she had rescued it from the *Swamp Fox* was pushing at me.

"All right, we can go now," I said.

On deck Clara turned to me. "You don't have to stay with me. It's best we separate. In about an hour they'll be letting some deck passengers off at Fairfield. With any luck, I'll have gotten to the captain by then and they'll put Nicholas off there, too." She smiled. "You can walk about in the snow."

Once again her boldness struck me. Only this time, favorably. She had a presence of mind far older than her years. Likely her hatred of Nicholas had something to do with it. But was that so bad? The safety of a hundred and fifty passengers was in the balance. To say nothing of Grandmother's cotton.

"Clara!" I felt the need to say something nice.

She turned and smiled at me. Her voice was muffled in the swirling snow. "Yes?"

"You're ready for Oberlin now," I told her.

She smiled and turned away.

We parted.

Through the swirling snow I saw that a thin crust of ice had begun to form in the distance on Long Island Sound. The whole world beyond the railing of the ship was a howling darkness. Wind blew across the deck, cold and biting, like no wind I had known at home.

There were a few passengers walking the deck, bundled in coats. I saw the lights in the wheel-house, up ahead, like a beacon in the dark. Two men were in there.

I was alone and cold. I ducked inside a door to a passageway where the wind could not get me. Then I smelled steam. I minded then that I was alongside the engine room.

Two men were walking by on the deck. They paused, just outside the door.

"Shouldn't even be out on a night like this, Captain," one said.

"Yes, but we advertised that we'd run at night."

"How are the boilers holding?"

"The engine generated fifteen inches of steam. I wanted the fires banked and the safety valves opened. But Marshall, the expert we took aboard in Manhattan, said not yet, that we won't be able to get through this ice. Says to wait until we get closer to Fairfield."

"Do you think he knows his business?"

"I wouldn't have sailed without him tonight."

The captain! Had Clara gotten to him? I should do something. But what? Tell him she was looking for him? How could I, a mere slip of a girl, approach a man who had such troubles this night? He'd laugh at me and send me to bed.

How could Clara approach him? Why should he listen to her outlandish story? He would believe the engineer.

". . . best get some rest, Captain," I heard his companion say as they moved away.

"Yes. I'll be in my cabin."

I watched them go. *Where was Clara?* I must find her and tell her the captain would be in his cabin. I went out again onto the deck. It was deserted now, but for some bulky figures in the distance. They must be part of the crew. No one who had the sense of a coon dog would be out this night.

I looked around me into the howling darkness. Overhead tall smokestacks belched snow-white vapor. *Chew, chew, chew.* I minded that the sound, and the steady beat of the paddles, had become part of my existence in a few short days.

Where was Clara? I waited about ten more minutes, ducking inside the passageway by the engine room to escape the wind, blowing on my hands, moving my feet, clutching my oilskin bag and reticule. My toes were frozen. Then, when I could bear it no more, I went back through the grand saloon.

I was surprised to see about a dozen people assembled there. And then I realized they were deck passengers, getting off at Fairfield. We would soon be there. It was where Nicholas was supposed to be put off, if Clara succeeded with her plan.

"About twenty more minutes," I heard a man say to his wife, as he consulted his pocketwatch. "Be patient, dear."

I went upstairs to our cabin. I would tell Elinora. There was nothing else for it. I must. Clara could be in trouble this very minute.

But our cabin was dark. I lit a candle and looked around.

Elinora was not there.

Likely she'd become worried about us and was out looking for us this very minute! I must find her.

Then I thought, no. I may not find her out

there in that howling darkness. I must go to the Ingrahams. Oh, how I dreaded it! How could I explain things? But I must.

Then I realized that I did not know the Ingrahams' room number. In all the confusion of boarding, Mrs. Ingraham had not told me.

I stood there pondering. It seemed like days ago, not hours, since we had come aboard. What time was it? Late. All the cabin passengers were settled in their rooms for the night.

I stood at the top of the stairs, looking down into the grand saloon. More people had gathered. I went downstairs, pushed through the people, and went out onto the deck. In the far distance, I could see pinpoints of light. Was it Connecticut?

"Clara!" I yelled.

No answer. Why were my bones so cold? I should go back upstairs and pack my other clothes. And my portmanteau, where I'd hidden all the money Grandmother had given me.

No, there wasn't time. I had all I could do, anyway, to hold on to what I was carrying.

Up ahead I saw only one figure — the captain. He was prowling the deck. I would approach him myself, I decided.

Just then he went through the passageway that led to the engine room. Then he opened the door and went in.

I followed. Inside the passageway I caught my breath. Should I knock? What would I say to him when the door was opened? "Captain, I must see you, please, there is an emergency." I would be polite. Politeness always worked with grown-ups. He had to pay mind to the concerns of his passengers.

I knocked once, twice. I pounded. The door opened.

The engine room looked like the bowels of hell, as Reverend McElheran tried to depict it for us.

Steam hissed. Men, stripped to the waist, were laboring over valves, rags in hand. Others were standing in front of the open furnace door, banking the coal fires.

"Open the safety valves!" the captain was yelling. "Reduce the steam eight inches!"

"Leave it at fifteen, Captain," yelled a burly, red-faced man, "and don't bank those fires yet, if you want to make port through this ice!"

"Eight, I say, Mr. Marshall. I know my ship!" the captain barked. "What kind of engineer are you?" Marshall! This would be Nicholas! Then the captain saw me. "Who are you? What do you want?" His face had the look of a man besieged.

"Captain, excuse me, sir. There's an emergency. I would speak with you."

Then the man they were calling Marshall caught sight of me. His eyes went over me quickly. He threw down the rag in his hand and pushed the captain aside. "What are *you* doing in *her* clothes? Where is she?"

I could see in an instant that he was not a man of good parts. There was the presence of evil about him. Did no one else see it?

"Where *is* she?" Nicholas bellowed at me again.

"Mr. Marshall," the captain's voice was full of authority, "what is this? This girl is one of my passengers. What have you to do with her?"

I didn't wait to hear what the man called Marshall would say. I only knew that I had to flee from him. All other purpose left me.

Next thing I knew I was running on the deck, through the darkness. Someone was running after me. I struggled to hold on to the oilskin bundle that held Grandmother's quilt. And the reticule with the Bible in it.

And it was as if some other darkness, worse than that which I found myself in, was rushing toward me to suck me into it.

Then, of a sudden, the darkness became light. And there was a great exploding sound. The deck beneath my feet shuddered. I heard the smashing of glass, the screams of people, the whooshing of steam. I was thrown across the deck and I landed against something. Hard.

Then everything went black.

In what seemed like a few moments, I came to again. I was on my hands and knees and the deck under me was hot and covered with broken glass. I was clutching the reticule, *but I had lost the quilt.*

Something was on top of me. It felt like a cushion.

I pushed it off. I struggled to get up. All around me was the sound of screaming and the crackling of flames. I smelled smoke. Men were yelling and rushing about.

I remember thinking, *Grandmother will lose all her cotton.*

And then, mercifully, there was blackness. And silence.

Chapter Eight

Grandmother's silence.

I know it was, because I heard her voice. "People cannot stand silence. They fear it like an abyss they may fall into. They fill in that hole with talk. . . . So you not only become strong, you learn the secrets of others."

But there was something Grandmother hadn't told me. Suppose you did not want to know the secrets of others? Suppose they turned out to be a burden to you?

Someone was shaking me, yelling into my ear. A man's voice. "You there, wake!" The sound worked its way into my ear. "Wake up, girl. Do you hear?"

I opened my eyes. Mercifully, I was alive. And clutching my reticule with Grandfather's Bible in it. Staring down at me was Nicholas.

All around me people were screaming and running. There was smoke and fire. Bells were ringing.

Men were yelling orders. Someone was bellowing, "Lower the longboats!"

None of it mattered. Only that Clara's terrible brother-in-law hovered over me, gripping my arm.

"Where is she? The girl whose clothes you're wearing. Clara. And her sister. My *wife*. Where are they?"

"I don't know, please, let me go, please, I must get to safety."

He gripped my arm tighter. "Don't know? How come you to be wearing her clothing?"

"I was traveling with her. We switched clothing. It was a lark. Then she disappeared." Oh, my head hurt. It hurt to talk. And my shoulder ached where I'd fallen on it.

"What's your name, girl?" He grabbed me roughly by both arms and drew me toward him. His breath smelled of whiskey.

I did not answer.

"You want to go to safety? You want to get off this boat with life and limb?"

I nodded dumbly.

"There's a longboat being lowered. I'll get you on it. Just tell me your name."

He pulled me to my knees as he said this, and pointed. And there I saw a large kind of rowboat being lowered into the water a short distance from us.

"Your *name*," he said again.

My life for my name. Even in my addled state I knew there was no real choice. "Amanda Videau."

"From where?"

"South Carolina."

"Sath Ka-lana, is it? Where you headed?"

"Lowell, Massachusetts."

"My wife is from Lowell. I figured she was going back. Why were you traveling with them? Never mind now. Just listen to me, Amanda Videau from Sath Kalana. You so much as breathe a word of what you saw tonight . . . that you saw me in the engine room, and I'll kill you. You hear?"

Surely, this man was from hell itself. Why would he kill me? I stared at him dumbly.

"The captain is dead," he said. "So's everyone else who was in the engine room. Far as anyone knows it was Mr. Marshall in there with them. You tell anybody that it was me, and I'll kill you. You *hear?*"

How could I not hear. He was screaming it at me. "Yessir."

"You open your mouth, when they come asking questions . . . you breathe a word about my being aboard, and you'll be dead."

Why didn't he kill me now? He looked as if he could do it with little or no effort.

Instead he pulled me to my feet and started dragging me to the boat that was about to be lowered over the side.

"My quilt!" I yelled. "I have to have my quilt!"

"You mean this thing?" He scooped Grand-mother's quilt up from where it lay in a heap a bit away from us on the deck. "This is *yours?*"

The oilskin bag had been torn open, either by the explosion or by him.

"Give it to me. It's my grandmother's!" I reached for the quilt that dangled in one of his hands, while his other hand gripped me.

"Your grandmother's? Then you're a Chelms-ford, are you?"

I stared at him crazily. People were pushing and shoving to get into the longboats, their clothing torn, their eyes dazed, their smoke-blackened faces stunned. And this unbelievable man was con-cerning himself with my lineage. As he knew it to be from the name he could see on the quilt in the firelight.

"Give it to me!" I screamed.

"A Chelmsford, are you? Well, well." He chuckled. "Good to know. My high-toned wife was always talking about them. Richest nabobs in New England. I'll just keep this quilt, if you don't mind, Amanda Videau from Sath Kalana. It could come in very handy."

He tucked it under one arm and shouted above everyone's head as he dragged me along. "I've a little girl here, needs to be put aboard. You gents, step aside. Step aside, I say, I'm from the crew! Captain's dead! I'm next in command!"

The bulk of bodies parted and he lifted me in the air.

"My quilt!" I yelled. "I want my quilt!"

"She's hysterical," he told the others in the longboat. "Look out for her." Then he dropped me in, leaned over, and whispered in my ear. "Only reason I'm saving you is that you're the link to my women. And I'll find you. And that rich relation of yours."

I had landed in the lap of a buxom woman. "Poor dear," I heard her say. "Here, hold onto me."

I looked around. The boat was filled with women and crying children. One woman was praying. Two others were injured. One looked dead, with blood pouring from her nose and mouth. A man was in the front of the boat, holding oars. As they lowered us through the darkness and the swirling snow, I heard the ropes creaking, the men's voices above, giving orders.

This is hell, I told myself, as overhead, on the great hulk of the riverboat, another explosion shook the air and there were more terrified screams. I must tell Reverend McElheran what it really looks like.

I wondered if Clara had gotten off. And Elinora. What had happened to them? And then again, I sank into the soft, cottony cocoon of Grand-mother's silence.

* * *

"Poor dear, she's still in the grip of it."

"Ssh."

"Does anybody know her name?"

"How could we know that? Who's to tell us?"

"She looks like she's from quality. They say there were some people of quality on the boat."

"No. The clothes she was wearing when she was brought in were not the finest. But still, she's very fine somchow. Over a hundred lives lost, Mr. Wakefield, the investigator, said."

"Think of it. Two longboats dashed against the rocks, and her clinging to a bale of cotton."

"How many others do you have here, Mary?"

"Three more upstairs. Mrs. Franklin down the road has another six."

"What did the doctor say about this one?"

"That she should be kept quiet. And she might come out of it soon. All the others have gotten their senses back. Mr. Wakefield was talking to them yesterday."

"What did he find out?"

"The investigating committee only knows that a special engineer was taken on in Manhattan to fix the boilers. A Mr. Marshall. They say he didn't do his job right and the boilers burst. His body hasn't been found yet, so they think he may have run off. He was seen putting this little one aboard the longboat first. Well, at least he did one good turn. Mr. Wakefield was wanting to question her yesterday. She wasn't fit."

"She doesn't look any more fit today. Come, Mary, you should eat. Keep up your strength. You've taken on a big responsibility here."

"Responsibility? It's a joy just to think that my husband and I saw them in time. And were able to pull them out of the water and save them."

I was home at Yamassee in front of a roaring fire in the parlor. And it was Christmas Day, bright and cold outside. Eessa May was playing Christmas songs on her violin.

I was hot. I must have caught the fever. Yet I shivered with cold. Someone was forcing me to drink some liquid. I took it. It was hot, but still it did not warm me. Likely I would never be warm inside again.

Then my father came downstairs. He held out the blue pills. "Take them," he said. "You know they're a good remedy."

I took them and swallowed. More liquid. I wanted to tell my father that the pills would do no good. That they were only a talisman, like the negroes' blue doors.

Then someone put something in my arms. It was warm and wiggly. And something licked my face with a wet tongue.

It was one of Melody's pups. It was so soft and

warm. Oh, I was so happy to be home again. I must open my eyes.

At first everything was a blur. Then I saw the puppy. It was black. But Melody had had no black pups. Whose puppy was this?

"See, I told you it would bring her around."

"You're a wonder, Mary."

A pleasant-faced woman was standing over me. "Hello. How are you?"

I felt a stab of disappointment, because I was not home. The soft feeling of the dream fell away like a goosedown comforter, leaving me raw, exposed. I did not answer. My head and shoulder ached like the devil himself was pounding on me.

I was about to answer her. Then I gathered myself in, for I heard two voices.

One belonged to Nicholas. "You tell anybody that it was me, and I'll kill you."

The other belonged to Grandmother. "There may come a time when your tongue gets you into real trouble. Or when your silence keeps you out of it."

The investigator wanted to question me. If I could not speak, I would not have to answer.

I shook my head dumbly at the woman.

I would, for now at least, take refuge in Grandmother's silence.

They accepted it. They said something about the accident causing it. And then, while they were talking, I felt a stab of fear. *My reticule.* It was gone! I searched frantically around me on the settee.

"Is this what you're looking for?" Mary asked. "You were clutching it when we found you." She handed me the oilskin pouch. Inside, the Bible was safe and dry, and Grandfather's letter with it.

"I looked for a name in the Bible, but there was none," Mary said.

I clutched it close. Then I remembered the quilt. Oh, I'd lost the quilt! Nicholas had it in his filthy hands. I felt the pain of the loss, deep inside me. I had failed Grandmother. All these years she'd managed to keep it. She'd rescued it from the storm-tossed *Swamp Fox*, only to have it lost now by me. I sank back on the settee, tears running down my face.

I slept and woke and slept again. Night came, then day and night again. Mary fed me, washed me, helped me to the commode. A doctor came and examined me. He said the bump on my head was healing, as he'd said on his first visit that it would.

He said my inability to speak was likely from shock. I needed rest, he said, and quiet. I was lucky.

Mary fed me some more, bustled about me, and kept a one-sided conversation going with me as she did her chores. She and her husband sat and read to me at night.

Their name was Hutchinson. And this was not Connecticut, it was Long Island. Old Field Point, to be exact, if anything could ever be counted on in my life to be exact again.

I did not want to count on anything again. All I needed was in front of me: a warm bowl of soup or a plate of some Yankee meat and potatoes, the puppy's wet nose, and my Bible.

Little by little I allowed myself to think of the wreck. I allowed fragments of the memory to wash over me, like a low tide. It was not, after all, something you could think about all of a piece. You had to take it in little doses like Daddy's blue pills.

I thought of Clara, as I'd last seen her on deck, smiling at me like some kind of vision in the swirling snow. I thought of the Ingrahams, Florence, Elinora. All the happy people I'd seen in the dining room. Where were they now?

When I could no longer bear such thoughts I stared out the Hutchinsons' large window, from my settee. Their farm ran right to the water, like our plantation at home. There were tall sea grasses all around. The house was pleasant, old, solid.

Then I'd think of home, of Ty and Garland, Daddy, Rob Roy, Eessa May, the servants, and the horses. And it would be even more painful than thinking of the wreck.

So then I'd cuddle the puppy and think of how I'd been rescued.

On the night of January thirteenth, the Hutchinsons had seen the terrible explosion four miles off shore. They had run outside, along with their neighbors, down the road and waited in the snow with lanterns for the longboats to come ashore.

Waves dashed up on the rocks. Winds howled. They built a fire in the sand while they waited. They watched the bales of cotton from the riverboat, floating in the water.

The two longboats broke against some rocks and crumbled in pieces. Several people drowned. Others clung to the boat timbers.

Mrs. Hutchinson said that I had grabbed a bale of cotton that floated past me. And clung to it.

Grandmother's cotton. Sea Isle cotton.

Somehow ten people, myself included, made it to shore. I was unconscious. All this I learned in the two days after I opened my eyes.

Neighbors came and went, looked me over, and made clucking noises. Mrs. Hutchinson's daughter, Anne, visited with a baby. I was allowed to hold the baby. Because they did not know my name, they called me Phoebe.

Some of Mrs. Hutchinson's other survivor-guests finally wandered downstairs to take meals in their dining room. They peered into the parlor at me. None recognized me. "There were one hundred and fifty souls on that boat," I heard one of them, an elderly man, say. "How could we know everyone?"

I was not surprised that the Ingrahams weren't amongst them. I wondered if they were at the house down the road.

On the third day, Elinora came.

It was about noon. I lay, watching the wind play through the distant sea grasses, with the puppy sleeping on my lap. There was a knock on the door. Mrs. Hutchinson went to open it. I heard her say, "Hello, Mr. Wakefield."

The investigator! I shrank back inside myself. I closed my eyes, pretending to be asleep.

And then I heard him introducing someone. "This is Mrs. Rhordan, one of the survivors. She's been staying down the road. First day on her feet. She wants to see if your Phoebe knows what happened to her sister."

Elinora was alive. I felt a thrill of joy. Tears came to my eyes. It was like seeing family. Then came the fear. How could I speak to her?

They came through the kitchen and into the parlor. "This is Phoebe," Mrs. Hutchinson said proudly of me.

I saw Elinora's broad, intelligent brow furrow. She opened her mouth to speak. "But it's . . ." then, seeing the pleading look in my eyes, she stopped.

"It's the name we gave her," Mrs. Hutchinson said. "Can't speak, poor child. Do you recognize her, Mrs. Rhordan?"

"No," Elinora said quickly.

"Well, Phoebe," the investigator said, "you're much improved from the last time I was around. Couple more days and maybe you'll be talking. Take your time, child. Rest. Don't be afraid. I'll leave you to visit, Mrs. Rhordan. Some timbers from the wreck have washed ashore and the committee will be examining them this afternoon."

He went into the kitchen with Mrs. Hutchinson.

"You're alive," Elinora said. "Thank God."

I nodded yes.

"They said your body washed up ashore, two miles down from this place. The purser, who is one of the survivors staying with the Franklins, identified it. By the coat with the ermine trim."

Clara, I thought. Oh God.

I saw that she knew. And the knowing was not a fresh grief to her, but something she had set her mind to for some days now. "I knew it was Clara when they told me the girl they found had dark hair. Yours is fair."

I nodded yes.

"I saw the look on your face before. You were begging me not to give you away. I don't know why, but it has something to do with why you and Clara changed clothes, doesn't it?"

I nodded.

"And Nicholas?"

I nodded again.

"He was on board. I saw him when I was looking for you two on deck. You must tell me," she knelt down beside the settee and whispered urgently, "just shake your head yes or no. Did Nicholas throw Clara overboard?"

I saw the anguish in her eyes, the dark circles under them. Dear God, is *that* what she thought? I must comfort her. I must tell her otherwise.

I took her hand. "I can speak, Elinora," I said. "I just can't let them know. Nicholas didn't throw Clara overboard. She was looking for the captain to tell him Nicholas was posing as the engineer and the boat was in trouble. Nicholas never killed her. So don't take her death on as your fault."

"But she's dead anyway." She sobbed softly. "And if he hadn't been following me, she wouldn't be."

"She's dead because the boilers were faulty," I said. "And because she tried to save the passengers. She would have it no other way. She's a real heroine, Elinora. She wanted it that way. So don't cry now, please. I need you."

She hugged me and dried her tears. "We need each other. Why must you pretend you can't speak?"

I told her then.

She absorbed my tale in stoic silence. She put her hands over her face. "That man is so evil.

How could I ever have loved him?" Then she drew strength from some inner wellspring. "Well, I mustn't think of myself now. Others have more troubles. The Ingrahams are dead. And their servant. And scores of others."

The Ingrahams dead! Not possible! Mrs. Ingraham would not stand for it! She would demand her money back! And what of poor Florence? She didn't even choose to go on the boat. It was part of her job! The unfairness stung me.

The weak January sunlight played across Elinora's wan face. "There will be a serious investigation. Too many lives were lost. Nicholas let you go only to find me. But you can identify him. We must get you away from here, to safety."

"How? Mrs. Hutchinson won't let me leave. She treats me as her own."

She thought for a moment. "I have it!" she said brightly. "I'll tell her you're my sister. You're Clara."

"But you said you didn't recognize me."

"I'll tell her I said that for Mr. Wakefield's sake. Because he told me how he wants to question you, and I want to get you home. Because you're in such terrible condition. I'll tell her that you need time to get well, so you will be able to speak and remember again. Are you game?"

I thought about it. "If we tell her you're taking me to Lowell, Mr. Wakefield may come find us. He knows Nicholas put me in the longboat."

She nodded. "Mrs. Hutchinson seems like a

good woman. I'll tell her I'll get in touch with Mr. Wakefield when you're better. That we need our privacy. For now. I'll swear her to secrecy about our whereabouts. She likes you. She'll do it. What say you?"

I said yes. I'd be Clara.

Chapter Nine

Elinora nudged me. "Amanda, we're in Lowell."
I opened my eyes.

Our carriage was going over a wooden bridge. The town lay before us, bathed in the last remnants of a lovely winter sunset. I saw church spires, houses, great hulking buildings, a silver river tinted with red.

It was a town encircled by hills, and they were covered with snow. As we went down into it, I saw it was a town of many shops: apothecaries, milliners, dry goods, tobacconists, churches, houses, a railroad. And always the river.

"This is Merrimack Street," Elinora said. "Oh, it's good to be home."

Some houses were small and brick and connected. I had never seen connected houses before. Others stood apart, with iron fences around them and great windows.

We passed one where the iron gate was open. The sun was gone now. It was dusk. But I could see statues on the frozen lawn. Steps went up to a, what? Raised verandah with a railing all around? I did not know what to call it. In front of a large window I saw an astral lamp, ruby red in color, glowing. A woman sat at a table by the lamp, reading.

I felt a great stab of loneliness for home.

"That's the agent's house," Elinora said. "He is the agent for your great-grandfather's mill. His name is Mr. Bruckland."

We turned a corner to go down another street. On one side were more red-brick houses. On the other side a canal, all lined with trees. And then I heard the sound, a great rumbling.

It came from the building ahead of us, an enormous, hulking building hovering over everything, fearful in its size, with a steeple tower. In the yard of this building were great lighted torches.

"What is that place?" I asked.

"The mill. The reason for life in Lowell."

"It looks like a fortress. Or a church."

"In a way, it is both," she said.

"Elinora!" A woman stood in the doorway of a small brick house. Behind her light spilled out, breaking the darkness with its comforting welcome. The woman came down the steps to embrace her sister. She was buxom and gray-haired, dressed spotlessly in black bombazine. "Oh, thank God, you're alive."

They wept in each other's arms for a moment or two. I heard them murmuring about "poor dear,

Clara, gone on to her heavenly reward." And "what Mama would say."

But these were New England women. And in time I was to learn that they dried their tears quickly and went about with life.

Now Emma looked at her sister. "When can we expect her home?"

"We must talk, Emma," Elinora said.

"You wrote that they found her body washed ashore. Or was that just to assuage my grief?"

"I'll explain," Elinora said.

Emma sniffed and nodded, picked up her skirts to go up the steps, then saw me. "Who is this?"

"She survived the disaster. She needs to stay with us a while."

"But that's not possible! You know the rules! No one but those on the corporation are to stay in this house!"

"You got permission for me and Clara to stay, didn't you?"

"Only because you were both to work in the mill."

"For now we can say she is Clara."

"But why would we do that?" Emma frowned. "You are up to something, Elinora."

"Yes, I'm up to something. Must we stand here and freeze? Or can we go inside and discuss it."

We went up the steps. "Have you gotten yourself into another dolorous situation?" Emma asked. "Won't you ever stop bringing home strays?"

"This stray," Elinora said, "is the great-granddaughter of Nathaniel Chelmsford. She's been hurt. Her head is still injured. And her shoulder pains her."

Emma gasped. You would have thought her sister had said I was the daughter of President Van Buren. Her eyes widened. "Come in, child," she said. "I have bread and meat and tea. And I'll get you some Bullard's Ointment for your shoulder."

In no time at all they had me in bed in a warm nightgown. Emma put ointment on my shoulder, then gave me a tray of food. I ate some, but my head hurt. So she gave me laudanum and bade me sleep.

I heard them whispering out in the hall.

"Does she speak?" Emma asked.

"Yes, but we've agreed that she shouldn't for now." She explained about Nicholas, his role in the wreck, his threat to me, and how the authorities wanted to question me. "And she shouldn't speak here, either, if she's going to pass as Clara. Her accent would give her away. Is there anyone in this house who remembers Clara?"

"No. In the year and a half she's been gone, we've had a whole new complement of girls. You're lucky in that. But none of this explains why you didn't claim our sister's body and bring it home."

"By the time I recovered from the disaster, she and many others were given proper Christian burials."

"We could still have her shipped home."

"We can't. We *mustn't*. Or you will have another dead sister to bury," Elinora told her. "And this child's death on our heads. I have Clara's. I don't need another. Neither the authorities nor Nicholas know where we are. We must keep it that way. Nicholas means us harm, Emma. Real harm."

"Well, this is an unholy kettle of fish." Emma's whisper was savage. "Our poor little sister!" Her voice broke.

"Perhaps someday we can bring her home," Elinora said.

"Very well, Elinora, very well. You have won me over again as you always do. But if I know you, you have something more in mind. What is it?"

They started going down the stairs, their whispers receding. I got out of bed and crept to the door, then into the darkened hallway. I peered over the bannister, listening.

"To go to the Chelmsford residence tomorrow morning. With the girl. She must be returned to her family. You yourself said we can't keep her."

"The timing isn't good. Ebie, the granddaughter, is gone. On a trip to England with her husband. And you know she serves as liaison between him and the agents and workers."

"He won't need a liaison to welcome his own great-granddaughter. It will work in our favor, Emma."

"How?"

"Think. Old man Chelmsford has been watching you like a hawk, ever since Plumy stood on that pump over four years ago and got the girls to strike because he was cutting wages."

Plumy? Who was Plumy? And they were talking about my great-grandfather cutting wages. I strained my ears to listen.

"Now don't bring up that business with Plumy," Emma said. "She's been behaving. She's been on the corporation four years now and has three girls under her."

"Are you telling me she isn't working for the ten-hour day? Look, Emma, I love Plumy. She's your daughter and my niece. But if she's caught plotting against the corporation, you'll be turned out of this place."

"God help us," Emma said.

"No, I intend to help us. Old man Chelmsford will be so happy to find out his great-granddaughter is alive, he'll forget what Plumy did. And he might be more disposed to improve this place and your lot, too. It could use improving."

"Not that old skinflint," Emma said.

I drew back from the bannister. Elinora was taking me to see my great-grandfather tomorrow morning!

I went back into the room and looked around at the low, slanted ceiling, the bare floor, the rows of small beds.

How many girls slept in this room? At home Eessa and I each had our own spacious quarters. Eessa wouldn't last two minutes in this place.

It was clean, yes, but so *barren*, so sad. How

could anyone stand living like this?

I thought of Clara, waving to me on the deck in the snow. Clara had given her life to help the passengers. Surely, I could go along with things and help Elinora and Emma.

Grandmother wanted me to help others, didn't she?

I got back into bed. Then I heard a great clanging. The bells. I got up and went to the window.

Then came another sound, that of machinery coming to a great, grinding halt. Then came the distant hum of human voices. And a river, a floodtide of humankind coming out of the doors of the mill under the torchlight.

Women, hundreds of them. All sizes and shapes, streaming out the gate, going in different directions. Many of them winding past this house. They reminded me of the incoming tide at home.

I stood staring at their bonnets as they passed below me. In the hall downstairs the clock struck seven. Were they just finishing their workday?

Our negroes at home finished earlier.

All these women worked for my great-grandfather.

Was Plumy amongst them? What pump had she stood on to incur my great-grandfather's wrath? What was a strike? What was the ten-hour day?

Several of the girls below were coming to our door. I stood in the dark, listening to their voices, muffled from below stairs. Then I heard Grandmother's voice. "Cabot's daughter Ebie and her husband run things for the old man. I want you to bring the quilt to her."

But I didn't have the quilt. And Ebie was away. So how would I fare tomorrow?

Questions swirled in my mind, which was just starting to feel the effects of the laudanum. I got back into bed and fell asleep.

Chapter Ten

The next morning my eyes flew open before first light as if Grandmother's macaw were sitting on my shoulder. I heard breathing.

When I looked, I saw it was from a room full of girls. Their breathing seemed an uneasy business. None went about it peacefully. One girl coughed in her sleep.

And no wonder! The room was freezing! The windows were so frosted I could not see out. To make matters worse, my head hurt, my mouth tasted like Daddy's blue pills, and I was frightened of what lay ahead for me this day.

How had I come to be in this cold, unsavory place, amongst strangers? I wanted to go home!

Then came a jangling of bells, loud enough to make me think I was in the mill yard. All around me the forms came to life.

One girl lit a lamp. Another stood on her bed and began to sing, stopping to cough twice. It was a deep and ominous sound. "Now isn't it a pity," she sang, "such a pretty girl as I, should be sent to the factory, to pine away and die."

"Hush, Lizzy, you'll hurt your throat," a tall, dark-haired girl said. "Anyway, can't you see we have a guest?"

Lizzy jumped off the bed. "I do see. Who are you?" She stood over me.

"It's Clara," the tall girl said. "My aunt Clara. You've heard me speak of her. She was visiting my aunt Elinora in Baltimore and they just returned. And she was in that horrible riverboat accident we heard of. So she can't speak and we must take care with her."

"How can she be your aunt, Plumy?" Lizzy scoffed. "She's just a little girl!"

"I know. My aunt is younger than I. But I don't call her aunt. How are you, Clara?" She leaned over me.

So this was Plumy. And they must have told her what was going on. The look in her eyes said that she knew about the deception. I nodded my head and smiled.

"Clara, Clara, are you from the Sahara?" Lizzy sang.

My head was pounding. I thought Lizzy rude and childish. But I liked Plumy on sight. She had star-brown eyes, a strong, round jaw, a ready smile, and a quiet presence.

"Leave her be," she ordered.

"I'll leave her be when you take your things off

my chifforobe!" Lizzy crossed the room in two strides to sweep a comb and Bible from a beautiful mahogany chifforobe.

"For shame, Lizzy! Pick them up!" It was clear that Plumy was in charge here.

Lizzy did so. "It's my chifforobe and you know how special it is to me," she mumbled.

"Get dressed, everyone, or we'll be late for breakfast," Plumy then advised the other girls. And all around me there was movement. "You must think them heathen, Clara," Plumy buttoned her dress as she spoke.

I shook my head no.

"Good. Lizzy only wants you to know that she earned the money for the chifforobe from the articles she published in the *Operatives Magazine*. She writes. Many of us do." She turned to Lizzy. "Take your tonic. Your cough is worse this morning."

"It doesn't help." But Lizzy took it anyway. There was a great hurrying then. Shoes were buckled, shawls and bonnets reached for. Even Lizzy rushed.

"Clemmie," a girl said. She stuck out her hand. She was very tall.

Plumy introduced her. "This is Clementine Averill."

I took it. It was the first time I'd ever shaken hands in my life. *Oh, how I wished I could speak.*

There were two others. Harriot Curtis and Lucy Larcom. Introductions were made. I looked into their faces. There was no fluttering of eyelashes, no tilting of chins, no lowering of eyelids, as girls did at home. They were all plainly dressed, but their movements and manner were certain, brisk, even regal.

I liked them.

"We must go. Breakfast doesn't wait," Plumy said. "We'll see you later. Why don't you rest a bit and come down for breakfast after the cattle have gone? There are several other girls in the house."

Hours later I walked down the snow-covered street with Elinora, to my great-grandfather's house.

It had been a morning to make my already aching head ache more.

Emma had sent a note to my great-grandfather's house last evening. After the mill girls left, I was taking my breakfast of flapjacks and tea with Elinora and Emma when a knock came on the front door.

It was a man with a message from the Chelmsford house.

It said we could present ourselves at two that afternoon.

"I *told* you, Emma!" Elinora fairly danced up and down. "You see?"

"What I see is a note signed by J. Solomon Aldrich. His lawyer," Emma said.

"Well, of course! Rich men have lawyers! He's

doing it proper-like." Elinora clasped the note to her bosom. "Oh, Amanda, how exciting!"

Emma looked the way I felt. Dubious. And I'd had enough excitement for a while, thank you. But I allowed Olive, Emma's only serving girl, to take me into the kitchen and give my head a wash with some evil-smelling soap and a vinegar rinse. The vinegar smelled terrible, and Olive was most thorough. I shivered in my shift and wondered if these people had ever heard of scented soaps or oils.

Then I was put in front of the fire to dry my hair while Emma and Elinora scoured the house for clothes suitable enough for me to be presented to my great-grandfather.

They found a silk plaid gown and a red woolen cloak. My hair was dried, the curls combed out and done up with a matching ribbon. I was given a fleecy woolen undervest, flannel pantaloons, and woolen stockings.

I would itch, but here in Yankee land certain sacrifices had to be made. I would be warm.

When the girls came home for their noon meal, I had mine. In the kitchen. Boiled turnips, cold mutton, relish, and tea. I could scarcely eat. *Well, I told myself, after today, all this will be over.*

Tonight I will likely be sleeping in a featherbed in my great-grandfather's house. I will dine on roast something, be given a silken robe, and have chocolate cake for dessert. So I ate.

"Must you carry that oilcloth pouch?" Emma

asked as she and Elinora inspected me after I had dressed.

We were out of earshot of everyone, so I could speak. "Grandfather's Bible is in it. And a letter from him. It will help to show my great-grandfather who I am."

"Why should he doubt it?" Emma asked.

I thought of the story Grandmother had told me about Thankful's daughter. *Do family legends and curses get handed down,* I wondered? "I had a quilt," I told them. "It had Grandmother's name written on it. She wanted me to give it to Cousin Ebie. But Nicholas took it from me on the boat."

"He *took* it?" Emma's eyes narrowed.

"Yes. He said it would come in handy someday. He knew of my great-grandfather."

Elinora groaned. "He heard me speak about the Chelmsfords. Oh, God. That means he knows who you are."

"Yes," I said.

Emma drew in her breath and glanced at her sister. "He can't be here in Lowell yet. Still, you'd best not waste any more time. Be on your way."

"I wish I had my quilt," I said to Elinora as we went out the door.

"And I wish Nicholas didn't have it," she said.

Elinora hurried through the snowy streets. She kept her head covered with the hood of her cloak, and crossed the street if anyone approached us.

And she chatted all the way.

I heard nothing of what she said. All I could think of was my great-grandfather.

Would he be glad to see me? What did he look like? Would he welcome me with open arms? What would his house be like?

I shivered in anticipation.

Then, finally at the end of Merrimack Street, across from the Congregational Church, Elinora stopped.

"There is the house," she said.

I looked. The house was elegant, made of fine stone. It was three stories high with a gracious portico in front. There was a round tower on one side, and the windows were long and draped with graceful fabric. The whole place was sealed off by a high wrought-iron fence. Lawns sloped on one side of the house down to the river.

There was a garden filled with bushes and trees of every shape and size. A neat brick pathway wound through it. Statues of cherubs sat guarding a small pond in the center.

"It's beautiful," I said.

"Yes."

And then I saw it. The front door. It had fine pilastered woodworking.

And it was blue.

The same blue as that on the negro cottages back home. I gasped.

"What is it?" Elinora asked.

"Nothing," I said. How could I explain? And

then I noticed something else. "The door is hung with crepe."

"It's for you," she said. "You're supposed to be dead."

Grandmother always said that our Episcopal church at home was like an exotic plant that developed under the sun of royal patronage in colonial times.

As I stood in the foyer of my great-grandfather's house, those words came to mind. Royal patronage. I did not exactly know what they meant, but they had a ring to them that fit the house. Royalty could have lived here.

Dark paneling, deep rugs, shining wood floors, massive doorways, heavy draperies, an aura of hushed elegance. Like a church.

A female servant in black silk with a lace cap and apron ushered us into a small parlor where a mantle clock ticked out the graceful minutes.

The maid left us. "Look at this place!" Elinora stood gaping. "Did you ever see such elegance?"

I shook my head no. Which was not true. If you wanted to fix your head with elegance, Grandmother's house had this one beat a country mile. And my daddy's house was no shanty, either.

As a matter of fact this place was dark, even forbidding.

The next moment we heard footsteps in the large foyer. I turned. There stood a man, tall, thin,

graying, well turned out in the style of the
moment.

He stepped into the room. "Ladies, I am Mr.
Chelmsford's solicitor, J. Solomon Aldrich. Mr.
Chelmsford is, ah, indisposed this afternoon and
asked me to meet with you. Please, do sit. I hope
to make this as painless as possible."

We sat. "He promised to meet with us," Elinora
said.

"The note said you could present yourselves."
J. Solomon Aldrich smiled. "He is an old man.
Ninety-three. We try to spare him these little
unpleasantries."

"*Unpleasantries?*" I thought Elinora would fall
off the chair. And, truth to tell, I wasn't doing
too well myself. I'd heard that word, unpleasantries, before. From one of Grandmother's lawyers.
I got a mite worried.

"What do you mean by painless?" Elinora asked.

J. Solomon sat and crossed his legs. And I got
more than a mite worried. I outright didn't trust
him. Down where I came from a man was considered peculiar-like if he crossed his legs.

"These things always get messy," he said. And
he smiled at me as he said it.

I knew then that I was ruined and done for.
Elinora didn't know it, but he was using all the
words I'd heard Grandmother say her lawyers used.

"What things?" Elinora fair croaked it out.

He sighed. "At least once a year we have something like this happen."

"Like what?" Elinora asked.

"Five years ago a man came to Lowell from England, claiming to be Richard Lander's grandson. Mr. Lander was married to Mr. Chelmsford's daughter, Hannah. They are both dead now. But Mr. Lander was world-traveled."

"She *is* his great-granddaughter!" Elinora said.

"Mr. Chelmsford retains many solicitors, such as myself, to shield him from such claims," J. Solomon said.

Dead silence in the room except for Elinora's gasp and the ticking of the clock. I thought of speaking up, but Elinora had said she would handle it. Elinora gathered herself in. I must say that for her. "This *is* Amanda Videau. In the flesh. She's come up from South Carolina to see Mr. Chelmsford, her great-grandfather. She was on the riverboat *Lexington* when the boilers blew. I and my sister were on the same boat. We made friends. By some miracle, Amanda and I survived. I brought her to Lowell from Connecticut, where we were rescued."

Like most lawyers, J. Solomon was prepared for us. "My dear lady, I am most gratified that you both survived. It was a terrible accident."

I just hate that, when people are nice to you and you know right well they're ready to stab you in the back. J. Solomon must have thought us a passel of fools. But I didn't say anything. Elinora had told me to let her do the talking.

"But we must stop all attempts at deception right now," he finished.

"There is no deception," Elinora insisted.

"I shall put it down to the shock of the accident," he said. "You see we have been warned that you would come like this."

"Warned?" Elinora's face went white. "Who warned you?"

J. Solomon's eyes fair glittered. "Your husband."

"My husband was here?" Elinora was near beside herself.

"Yes, madam. He told us he is looking for you. His wife, who ran away with her sister. He told us how Amanda's body was recovered after the wreck and the purser identified it by the coat with the ermine trim. And she was buried in Connecticut."

"It's a lie!" Elinora burst out. "All of it."

"A lie?" he raised delicate eyebrows. "Are you not, then, the wife of Nicholas Rhordan of Baltimore?"

"I am."

"Did you not *desert* him?"

"I left him. He is a cruel husband. And that body that was identified in Connecticut was my sister. She and Amanda changed clothing just before the accident. My sister did it to elude him."

"Madam, please," he said.

"It's true, all of it! Oh you must believe me." She bit her lip. Tears came to her eyes. Then she had a thought. "She has a Southern accent. Talk to the man, Amanda. Go ahead."

"Everything she's said is true, sir. I have my grandfather's Bible to prove it." And from inside my cloak I took the oilcloth pouch. I withdrew the Bible and showed it to him.

He waved it aside. "Mr. Rhordan said you became close with Amanda on the trip. Likely you took the Bible."

"I don't steal, sir," I said.

"You see how she speaks?" Elinora asked him. "She doesn't say I. She says ah."

Again he waved her away. "The young are wicked good mimics."

I thought of something, then. "He took my quilt," I said. "Grandmother gave it to me. It has her name on it. I was bringing it to my great-grandfather."

"He showed us no quilt, young lady."

"But he *took* it. For his own gain. And that's how he knew who I was and that I would come here. If he hadn't taken it I could prove who I was."

He was quiet, calm, even placating. "But you don't have it, do you, this mythical quilt?"

I wanted to scream at him. I wanted to get up and cross the room and slap his face. But instead all I could say was, "No, sir, I don't have it."

"Then why don't we end all this peaceably now? Before it gets ugly."

"Ugly?" Elinora asked. "Are you about to threaten us, sir?"

"I am about to cite the laws in this state which uphold the right of a man to claim his wife. Wherever he finds her."

"You are threatening me," Elinora said.

"I do not threaten women," J. Solomon said with great dignity. "I only cite the law. If you do not go peaceably, I shall be forced to let your husband know of your whereabouts."

I saw the breath go out of Elinora, as if she had received a terrible blow. "Certainly in the name of decency, you would not do that. The man intends us harm."

"I do not particularly care for your husband, madam, which is why we made the decision not to tell him where you are. We could have, at the outset, you know."

"You didn't tell him so you would have a threat to hold over me," Elinora said.

"Think what you will, madam. I must protect Mr. Chelmsford. Furthermore, he is fully aware that your niece started the first strike against his mill some years ago now. He was lenient with all of you that time. But I am afraid that if you give him more trouble, he will not be averse to ending your sister's tenure at the boardinghouse."

Elinora nodded her head woodenly. "I see." She gathered her gloves and reticule. "Come, Amanda, let's go."

I got up. "I'll contact my daddy," I said. "He'll write to my great-grandfather and tell him who I am."

But J. Solomon was ready for that, too. He stood, hands clasped behind him, rocking back and forth. "I would not do that if I were you. Mr. Videau was told of his daughter's death. We were informed he had a seizure. Writing to him could kill him." He took a step toward me and peered into my face. "If you *are* his daughter, as you claim, you wouldn't want to kill him, now, would you?"

I was trapped. "No, sir."

"So then. If we receive any letters from South Carolina, you will only weaken your cause. And in that case, I shall certainly be obliged to tell Mr. Rhordan of your whereabouts."

I felt like a fox in a legtrap. Like I was wandering, lost, in the sea grasses at home. Or marooned on the mudflats with the tide coming in. Nowhere to go. Oh, he was a lawyer, all right. I felt helpless rage course through me.

"Let's go now, Amanda," Elinora took my hand.

I went with her into the foyer. The maid appeared and showed us to the door. I had another thought then. "I know why this front door is blue," I said.

He sighed and raised his eyes to the ceiling. "Have your say, miss, if it will make you happy."

"It's the color of the doors on the negro cabins at home."

"It is blue on the whim of Mrs. Ebie. Who is not here, thank heaven. It has been blue for years."

Elinora tugged my arm. "Enough, Amanda. Come now, let's go back to the boardinghouse."

"Ah, yes," J. Solomon stepped into the foyer. "That is another matter. The girl is staying in the house with you then."

"Where would you have her go? In the street?" Elinora asked.

"Certainly not, madam. She is your sister. But even so, if she is to reside in the house, she must work in the mill. You are aware of the ruling?"

Work in the mill? I stared at Elinora. Then at this popinjay of a lawyer. Work in the mill? My daddy would shoot him first!

I opened my mouth to speak.

Elinora grabbed my arm and pulled me out the door. "We are aware of the ruling," she said.

We went outside into the cold. The blue sky seemed to swirl above me. The glaring whiteness of the snow hurt my eyes. I felt dizzy. But Elinora pulled me down the steps of the portico and along the front path.

"He can't do that to us," I whispered savagely, "he can't."

"He can. We have no proof of who you are. Nicholas got here before us. You heard him. He's going to tell Nicholas where we are if we don't go peacefully. Now come along."

She was frightened. Her face was white. Her

hand trembled. We went out the front gate. As we started down the street, I turned.

Why I looked up, I don't know. But in a second-story window, I saw the curtains part, saw a man looking out at us. An old man. *Great-grandfather!*

Why was he watching us? To make sure we went? To see what I looked like? I felt so wretched. I kept my head turned, looking at him as I stumbled after Elinora on the street.

Now I knew how Peggy felt that morning, being led away by Mr. Tribley while Daddy watched, saying nothing.

So much for my chocolate cake, I thought crazily. So much for featherbeds. So much for my great-grandfather.

Chapter Eleven

The next morning I stood next to Emma. In the mill.

I still could not believe I was here. It was all a bad dream, surely. I would wake soon and find myself back in my room in Yamassee. The nightmare would be over.

Emma mouthed some words and pointed to a man talking with a young woman in front of a large machine. I could not hear a word she said, but I took it that the man was Mr. Schell, the overseer.

She was waiting to speak to him.

The noise was unbearable. How could anyone endure it? There was a constant banging and scraping and clanging. And I was in the middle of it. Me. Amanda Videau, daughter of privilege, who'd been cosseted all her life. *They expected me to work here.*

I was not only dumbfounded, but numb with cold and nauseous. I hadn't been able to eat the mush they called breakfast, so early, in a room full of chattering girls, with the dark beating against the windows outside.

I wanted hominy, sugared ham, fresh fish, pots of good coffee or chocolate, sweet buns.

My head hurt because I'd scarcely slept, but turned and tossed all night, while voices, faces, and visions haunted my brain. What of Daddy? A seizure? Surely Doctor Fripp wouldn't allow anything to happen to him. Oh, I hoped Daphne would attend to him properly. Would Eessa May do it, if Daphne failed? I wondered if Daddy would take his blue pills. Oh, he could not be sick! He was the one who nursed all the others, family and servants when they fell ill. Surely, he would recover!

I had decided I should not write to him, but give him time to get well. We had talked late into the night, me and Emma and Elinora, after everyone else in the house was asleep. We had talked the thing through. I thought they would never make an end of it. Then I finally decided

There was nothing for it but for me to go on pretending to be Clara and work in the mill. Or else I'd be in the street. So now I stood next to Emma in the ungodly cold, dumb with shock and grief. So much for Grandmother's North.

We'd heard about the mills up North. I'd grown up knowing that everything they did in the North was tainted with greed and vulgarity. Besides which, they put tariffs on us. Once I asked Daddy what a tariff was. He said it was an abomination. That everything about the North was an abomination.

"No," Grandmother told him, "don't tell the child that. The gentle bond of old associations must not be broken."

I stood amid the clamor, the confusion. Another version of hell. They certainly served up a variety of them here in Yankee land. And I thought, *This is gentle? You were right, Daddy. It is an abomination.*

"This is the carding room," Emma yelled at me.

It was very bright. There were many plants in the windows. But you could see things flying through the air, bits of cotton. It settled on the hair of the girls attending the machines.

In five minutes it settled in my throat.

The space between the machines was not very wide, but the young girls were all lithe and dashed about, reaching their hands into the very jaws of the machines. Any minute I expected one of them to lose a hand. But it didn't happen.

Finally Mr. Schell came over and gestured to follow him into the hall where the noise abated somewhat. But the floor under us shook just the same.

"Is she healthy?" He had to yell the words.

"Of course," Emma yelled back.

"No cough?"

Emma was offended. "I don't allow anyone with a cough in my house."

"They all cough," he said. "Why is this one any different?"

"She is my sister."

"Why doesn't she speak?"

Emma launched into the story of the riverboat wreck.

All the while he eyed me. "Can she hear?"

"Of *course*." Emma was indignant.

He laughed then. "Blessing if she couldn't, hey? Come here, girl." He gestured that I should step forward. "Open your mouth," he said. And then he inspected my tongue, my teeth.

I had seen Daddy do this with our negroes, Rob Roy to the horses. Tears came to my eyes.

"She's too old to be a doffer," he told Emma.

"Don't you have an opening in the weaving room?"

He scowled. "Do you think," he yelled, "that you could learn to thread the shuttles and tie weavers' knots? They lost a girl in the weaving room last week."

He might as well have asked if I could learn to hunt a bobcat. But I nodded yes. I smiled, as Emma had instructed. I could learn anything. For a while. For I intended to write immediately to Grandmother and have her rescue me.

Learning would not be the problem, I decided.

— *137* —

Forgetting this place once I was out of it would be.

They took me to another room and set me to threading shuttles. They gave me a loom. They had more than enough to give. The room was filled with looms. And girls. All sizes of girls who moved about tending two or more machines.

"This is Moria Hamilton!" Mr. Schell yelled. Then he yelled my name at her. So much for introductions. "Moria will teach you!" In the next moment he was gone.

I'd noticed Moria in Emma's house. She was a quiet type and she had a nervous blink. It's a wonder they all didn't, I decided. Moria smiled at me and nodded. She was tall and long-faced. She looked to be in her twenties. "There's more thread on the warp beams than we have weavers to handle it!" she yelled into my ear.

I nodded, as if I understood the problem and had always considered it one of life's major vexations.

"Watch me," Moria yelled.

She threaded the shuttle. Then she grinned, confidently.

I nodded and smiled.

"These are filling threads," she screamed at me. "They get woven into the warp threads. When they break you have to tie knots in them. Here, see?" And she tied one.

I did not see. Her fingers were so nimble.

"There's one broken now. You try."

I leaned over the loom. Couldn't they just turn it off so I could tie the knot? I picked up the thread and tried to tie it, but I couldn't make the two ends reach. Every time I got a grip on it, the machine did something to jostle the thread out of my fingers. And they were so stiff!

She took it from me. "The warp threads are starched before they get put into the loom, so that makes it difficult. But it can be done. There." And she blinked twice at me.

"Now you just watch your threads, don't take your eye off the machine for a minute. You'll do fine." She went to tend her loom. No, she tended *three* looms. She moved back and forth between them like a butterfly. Always, her hands were reaching into their innards. Her feet were never still.

I felt panic rising in my breast. They expected me to do *this*? All day?

Surely they were joking. Nobody did this all day. The noise alone was enough to drive one to distraction in five minutes. I took a quick look about. All around me, young girls were tending two, even three looms at once. Their arms reached and their bodies stretched as if in some fearful minuet.

The machines were their dancing partners. There seemed to be an awful liaison between the two. I was gripped by a thought. The machines could not work without the girls. And the girls could not work without the machines.

It was a terrible thought. Who had formed this unholy union?

It was clear to me from the start who had the upper hand here. It wasn't the girls. You didn't have to watch long before you knew that they'd lost their *selves* to a *thing*, with claws and teeth and insatiable wants.

"Watch that warp thread! It's broken!" Moria leaped over, stepped in front of me, and reached for the dangling, flapping thread. Expertly, she tied it. Then she turned on me. "You must be careful! You'll ruin the cloth!"

I nodded and wiped tears from my eyes.

"Stand with me," she said. "Watch everything I do. You'll learn. Everyone does."

I stood all morning, watching Moria while she tended three looms and taught me all at the same time. The world narrowed around me. I was vaguely aware of other girls doing a similar grotesque minuet on the outer edges of my vision. But all that mattered was the loom, with its quick, jerking movements and its endless demand for threads.

Its clacking became part of the rhythm of my own blood.

By the time the bells rang for our noon meal, my heart was beating in tune with the clacking. And I had learned to tie a warp thread. That was no mean feat.

Moria beamed. "Come on, we've half an hour to get home, eat, and get back." She led me out of the room and down the stairs.

I did not have to be led. I was like a drum fish, running in our creek during spring migration, being pushed along by the other drum fish who were all swimming the same way. Because if they didn't, they might lose their lives.

The thought of losing my life was not as peculiar as it might seem. Out in the factory yard, I was hit with the possibility of it.

In a far corner of the yard, I saw Nicholas.

I gasped. Here was the man who wanted to kill me. And who, if he chose to, could tag me, the way he'd tagged Clara, and make me like stained Sea Isle cotton.

He was leaning against a post, lighting a cheroot, all the while scanning the passing girls. I looked around for Elinora. She worked in the spinning room. I hurried along, head down, surrounded by the other girls, hoping Elinora had protective cover, too.

Out on the street, I turned once to look back. Nicholas was still standing there, searching the passing sea of faces.

He had not sighted us.

I was trembling when I got back to Emma's, but I went to sit down at the dining-room table.

Everyone set to eating, right off. There were no preliminaries, no niceties. Bowls were passed, plates and silverware clanked, food was shoved into mouths. Elinora saw me from a table across the room and smiled. I smiled back weakly.

My hands had tremors from the vibrations of the loom. I could still hear the clacking and whirring. But for the moment I was grateful for the surrounding bodies. Nicholas couldn't hurt me here. But shouldn't I tell Elinora I had seen him?

"Eat," Moria whispered to me.

The food was more boiled turnips and cold mutton. I yearned for Grandmother's creamed fish. These people did not know anything about food or nourishment.

"You must eat or you won't get through the afternoon," she whispered. "If you don't work your sister can't keep you on the corporation."

My sister? What did Eessa May have to do with this? Then it all came back to me. I was Clara. They had buried Amanda. It was a strange feeling, being dead. I wondered if Eessa May had cried very much. How Ty and Garland had taken it.

I was Clara now. I could not go home. At least not for a while. I had to go back into the mill again this afternoon and toil until after dark. I was trapped like a buck driven into the water by one of Daddy's dogs. And every time that happened to them, they drowned.

The bells rang me out of my reverie. "Come *on*," Moria said, "we'll be late." I followed her out into the cold. By evening when we returned to the house in the January dark, I was all used up.

My head pounded. My shoulders ached. My feet were swollen. I went right to bed, without even taking supper. If someone had offered me J. Crosby's Compound Bitters, I would have been beholden to her for the rest of my life.

Chapter Twelve

I know it was a foolishment on my part, but I didn't write to my grandmother for that whole first week.

The trap I was in held on all sides. I had to work in the mill because I had no money and no place to go. And when I got home at night I was so spent, writing was the last thing on my mind.

My body hurt all over. I could not sleep in that small, cramped, dismal room, for Lizzy's coughing at night. It seemed that every time I dozed off she would wake me again with that dry, hacking sound.

Beyond Plumy's admonishing her to "take your tonic," nobody took any mind of it. But I knew that if one of us had such a cough, Daddy would long since have sent for Doctor Fripp.

Finally, on Friday evening, when the other girls went out to lectures and improvement circles, I asked Emma for pen and paper, and in the quiet of the parlor, I wrote:

Dear Grandmother: I do not know how to begin this letter, except to say that I am alive. It is I writing, your Amanda. Do not believe what anyone has told you about my being dead. I am very much alive and living in Lowell. Only not with Great-grandfather.

You heard, of course, of the wreck. And that I was washed ashore in Connecticut and buried there, with others who met a similar fate. But that is not true. The body identified as mine was wearing my clothing. But it was a girl named Clara. We had become friends, I had traveled with her and her sister Elinora. They were fleeing Elinora's husband, Nicholas, who is even more a no-count than Lillienfield and twice as much grief.

Nicholas was following them and came aboard at Whitehall Slip in Manhattan, like the sly piece he is, pretending to be a special engineer who was to fix the ailing boilers.

Well, Clara saw him and asked me to switch clothing with her, so she could get to the captain and tell him the man posing as an engineer was not one. And the boat was in danger. Then off the coast of Connecticut the boilers blew and so we had disaster.

Grandmother, I saved the Bible. And your quilt. I had them with me, since I had the scent of trouble. But Nicholas found me after the explosion, then bullied me into telling him where Elinora, Clara, and I were going. He was all mooded up. Just like one of Daddy's hounds chasing wildcats to keep in shape for running deer.

He took the quilt. Because it had your name on it. He said his high-toned wife was always talking about the Chelmsfords and it would come in handy.

Well, Grandmother, it did. For him. He got to Great-grandfather's like the crow flies. The day after we arrived Elinora and Emma, her sister who runs the house here, got me all fancied up and Elinora took me there, but it was too late. Great-grandfather's lawyer was waiting and mouthing things you would be beside yourself to hear. Nicholas had gotten there first and poisoned their minds by telling them Elinora would come with Clara, pretending she was me.

The lawyer threatened to tell Nicholas where we were, if we persisted with my claim. And Elinora is more frightened of him than a mouse is of a hooty owl. We had to leave and go back to the boardinghouse.

Well, I was as fired up as Daddy was when the Major shot his cattle for going into his fields.

But what could I do? I came back to the boarding-house, where I am now and where I must act as Clara. Because no one can stay here unless they're "on the corporation," which means working at the mill. And that's the way they got me in here in the first place. Saying I was a dead person.

Which means I can't talk. Oh, Grandmother, to think you made me keep my silence for two weeks! Do you have uncommon powers? Did you know something like this would happen? Because my silence is serving me well. It may even save my life.

You see, first I couldn't talk because it was the only way I could get into the house. Because Clara would *talk like a Yankee. Now I must keep up the pretense. Because there is an investigation about the wreck, and I am the only one who can prove Nicholas was responsible.*

They are protecting me, Grandmother. You would love Emma. She looks well to the ways of her household. She and Elinora treat me like kin. Yet my heart is heavy. I must work in the mill in order to justify my stay here. It is back-breaking work. The mill girls toil longer hours than our negroes. My feet are swollen so that I can't tie the laces of my shoes, my fingers hurt, my head throbs, and my shoulders and back ache all the time. The noise is enough to burst my blood vessels.

Only you can rescue me. I cannot write to Daddy. Great-grandfather's lawyer said he was ill and news of my being alive (if I was who I claimed to be, and the lawyer didn't believe it) would kill Daddy.

I am addressing this to the nuns in Baltimore, since I figured you would still be there. I hope you are recovered and this has not been too much agitation for you. I miss home. I miss the boys and Eessa May and Daddy, Melody and the pups and Rob Roy and visiting your house. I miss the food sorely. The climate here is dreary. The town is full of tiny houses and ugly buildings. There is no green, no sand. I miss the smell of the water and the sea grasses, the sound of the wind, the tides, the hooty owls at night, the food, your tarot card readings, Brister's fiddle, everything.

Please send me some money so I can make the journey home. Please don't think of making the journey

North yourself. Yankee land is horrid. Write to Emma, not me. I cannot alert anyone to my presence here. Besides endangering myself, it would endanger Elinora. Nicholas is still looking for her.

Oh, yes, the Ingrahams are dead, lost in the wreck. And oh, Grandmother, I feel so grievous bad that I lost your quilt. Please forgive me. Your loving granddaughter, Amanda Videau.

Chapter Thirteen

February 1841

The second week, things got a little better for me.

No, I still could not abide the bells that jarred me awake at five each morning, to stumble about in the bone-numbing cold, aching from the day before and a night on the narrow lumpy mattress. Only to become nauseous again at the mush they served for breakfast. And the prospect of another day at the mill.

I still could not thread the shuttle or tolerate the noise. But I had tied a broken warp thread. I had to learn, I'd decided. If only for Moria. She was being so patient with me. And I could not allow her to continue doing my work.

The second week I began to sort out and understand the girls I lived with. They were divided into two groups. In one group was Harriot Curtis, Lizzy Turner, Lucy Larcom, Clementine Averill, Elinora, and Plumy.

Moria belonged to the other group, the girls

who went out almost every night to lectures and improvement circle meetings.

Ours was considered a "literary house." Plumy and her friends all wrote for the *Operatives Magazine*.

I soon discovered that this was not to be confused with the *Lowell Offering*, another magazine written by the mill girls. Plumy and her group criticized the *Offering*.

"It's a house organ for the mill managers," Plumy said.

I was confused. I knew what an organ was. But what did that have to do with a magazine?

Everyone was ahead of me, it seemed, speaking some language I did not understand. But I did know one thing. If our negro servants at home had meetings like the one I was invited to, it would be considered an uprising. And the inhabitants of St. Helena's Island would take to sleeping with their guns again.

At supper on Wednesday of the second week, Elinora sat next to me at the table. "Why don't you come into the best room with the other girls tonight? The way you've been going to bed right after supper, they think you don't want to be friends."

I looked around. Moria's group had left for a lecture. Plumy's group were all smiling at me. I nodded.

The best room was the fancy parlor, used by the

girls when they had male visitors. But few males came during the week to call. So the girls used it for their "social meeting." Here was a piano, a carpet, books, and periodicals.

Harriot Curtis closed the sliding doors and made room for me on the settee.

"You're in the place of honor," Lucy Larcom said. "Harriot's grandmother claims direct descent from Miles Standish. She's going to write an article about it for the *Operatives Magazine*, aren't you, Harriot?" Her voice was teasing.

"I may not be the poetess of Lowell as you are, Lucy," Harriot retorted, "but I've better things to write about."

Was there jealousy here? There were more undercurrents in this room than in Grandmother's house when Lillienfield came to visit.

"Anyway," Harriot insisted, "what I think we all ought to concern ourselves with tonight is the letter Clementine is writing to Senator Clemens."

"I've already written it," Clementine said. "What I need is for others to hear it. I'm going to send it to the *New York Tribune*."

A murmur of approval from the others. I listened in astonishment. Where I came from, women did not write letters to senators. Or publish those letters in newspapers. Where I came from the female got her name in the newspaper when she was born, when she married, and when she died.

Harriot turned to me. "Senator Clemens of Alabama stood on the floor of Congress and said that the life of the Southern slaves was better than the life of us girls here in the New England mills."

I thought of Peggy, hands bound, begging Daddy not to sell her.

"I think this is not the time to write such a letter," Elinora said. "Not the time to draw attention to this house."

"And when is the right time, pray?" Harriot asked.

Elinora did not reply. She seemed more nervous and withdrawn every day. I had told her about Nicholas looking for us in the mill yard. Perhaps I shouldn't have.

"Clemmie's letter won't draw Nicholas to you, darling," Plumy told her. "You're safe here with us. We'll protect you."

I thought it odd that Plumy should call her aunt darling. But it soon became obvious Plumy was the stronger of the two.

She turned to Harriot. "You know when the time is right," she said fiercely, "to draw attention to us. And it has nothing to do with Elinora."

"I know *you* think it's when we get enough signatures on the ten-hour petition," Harriot argued. "But that isn't what everybody else thinks."

Plumy looked around the room. "Is anybody here not in agreement with me? Don't you think that if we draw attention to ourselves before we present the petition, we'll be regarded as troublemakers? And then no one will pay mind to our petition?"

The other girls were silent. It was clear they were afraid to go against Plumy.

"We're regarded as troublemakers in this house now," Harriot told her. "You gave this house that reputation, Plumy, if you remember."

"That was four years ago, before any of you were here. But my actions were for a good cause. Again, I say, don't take action until the moment is right."

Lizzy Turner raised her hand then.

"Yes, Lizzy?" Plumy asked.

"I've seen Clementine's letter, Plumy. And, if anything, she's defending our life and lot here. Which is why I think she should send it to the newspaper. If anything, you'll see that it will put the mill managers at ease about us."

"If she's *defending* it, she should send it to the *Lowell Offering*," Plumy said derisively. "They'll love one more article telling how lucky we are to slave away thirteen hours a day."

"Hush, Plumy," Lucy Larcom spoke up then. "Let's hear the letter."

Everyone agreed. So Clementine read her letter.

It was very long. As Lizzy had said, it praised the pay the girls received for their labors, it spoke of good care when the operatives became sick. It said that most of the factory girls eventually married. It spoke of glorifying God by aiming for perfection in their work habits.

Clementine finished reading. " 'Have the slaves our privileges? By giving two weeks' notice we can leave when we please. We are allowed to visit friends, attend any school, or travel. Some of us have visited the White Mountains, Niagara Falls, and the city of Washington. Can the slaves leave when they please and go where they please? Shame on the man who would stand up in the Senate of the United States and say that the slaves are better off than the operatives of New England!' "

Everyone applauded lightly.

"Why do you wish to send such a letter, Clemmie?" Plumy asked.

"I know we're fighting for better working conditions," came the reply, "but I think we must have our pride."

Plumy nodded. And something came clear to me. These girls might fight amongst themselves, but they tried to understand one another. They protected one another.

They were family. And everyone had a say.

"Let's have a vote," Plumy said. "Should the letter be sent to the New York newspaper? Or does it go against what we are fighting for, our ten-hour workweek?"

Scraps of paper were set out. One by one the girls cast their votes. They smiled at me, encouraging me to follow.

Vote? I'd never done such a thing in my life! The idea intrigued me. I wrote "yes" on the paper and folded it neatly. I was gratified that they had included me.

Plumy counted the votes.

The yesses outnumbered the nos. Clementine's letter would be sent to the *Tribune*.

"A good night's work," Plumy told them. "But now I'm afraid we must get to more serious matters."

I sat benumbed. What could be more serious?

"We only have twenty names on our ten-hour petition," Plumy told them. "All the girls in the mill know that signing it means immediate dismissal. What they don't understand is that if we sign it, we can't all be dismissed. They can't run the mills without us. We could shut them down."

No one said anything.

Plumy went on. "We need to get the signature of someone the girls all look up to, someone whose lead they'll follow. Does anyone have any ideas?"

Silence. Then Clementine raised her hand. "What about Nancy?" she asked.

No one said anything for a moment.

"Don't you see?" Clementine asked. "The girls look up to her. She's been here forever."

Plumy laughed. "Nobody even speaks to her."

"You mean she won't speak to us," Harriot corrected.

"Why should she?" Plumy asked, "she has everything she wants. She comes and goes as she pleases. Why should she care about our problems?"

"She works thirteen hours a day, too," Harriot said, "maybe more."

"Because she *wants* to, not because she *has* to," Plumy said. "I heard she even sleeps in there sometimes."

"That was before they gave her a man to guard the place," Lucy said.

"No one is allowed in the print works," Harriot whispered to me. "Old man Chelmsford is afraid the art will be stolen. Nancy designed the first calico, years ago, with a print and color that would last. It was an indigo with a tiny white spot sprinkled in it. It made Chelmsford's reputation in the business. Before that, nobody could make a calico print that didn't wash out."

"If you ask me," Plumy put in, "I think the mystery attached to the print works is all so much nonsense made up by Nancy to make her seem important to old man Chelmsford."

"She is important to him," Lizzy reminded her. "Remember, she's related."

I felt a curious sensation on the back of my neck. And the thought that had been half formed in my mind became whole.

This Nancy they spoke of was the daughter of Grandmother's sister, Thankful. I was sure of it. Hadn't Grandmother said she had a position of importance in the mill? A shiver went through me.

"Well," Clementine said, sighing, "she has twenty girls under her in the dyeing room. She's very protective of them. And they have the same working conditions we have."

"She cares about her girls," Harriot said. "And I heard the reason she doesn't like us is because she thinks we have pretensions."

"She should talk," Plumy snorted, "the way she struts about. You'd think they couldn't run the place without her."

"Likely they couldn't," said Lucy. "Although, I heard she hasn't come up with a new design for the new calico print. And the old man is pushing her for one."

Plumy studied Lucy. "Do *you* think it would be a good idea to approach her?"

"Yes," Lucy said.

"Everyone?" Plumy asked.

The yesses were unanimous.

She turned to Lizzy then. "Tell them what happens every day when you bring one of our finished bolts of cloth to the print works."

"I have to knock twice and leave it outside the door," Lizzy said. "We're not even good enough for her to open her precious blue door to us."

Had she said blue door? I felt a start, like a hand on my shoulder. Everyone was talking at once now.

"Sometimes I'm afraid the cloth will be stolen after I leave it," Lizzy was saying. "And we're responsible, you know, if it is."

"I heard that she looks down on us because we make so much noise when we file in and out of the building," Clementine suggested. "She stood there one day and yelled at Livvy Broadhurst that we were all a bunch of cackling geese. And that where she comes from only one person speaks at a time. And the others listen."

"Where's *that?*" Lizzy asked.

"From the Ohio territory when she was a child," Plumy said. "She's supposed to be half-Indian. What does she *expect?* We can't hear ourselves think all day. Of course the minute we get out of our machine room we all talk at once."

"I suppose she'd like us to be mute," Harriot said.

Everyone fell silent and looked embarrassed.

"I'm *sorry,*" Harriot said. "I didn't mean to insult you, Clara."

"You can be an idiot sometimes, Harriot," Elinora said.

"Hush, all of you," Plumy ordered.

They hushed.

Plumy was looking at me. "Maybe she *would* take to someone who couldn't speak."

I heard the other girls draw in their breath.

"Plumy, you're *brilliant*," Lizzy gushed.

"Wait a minute," Elinora said. "Clara is new here. She's still getting used to the loom. It's fearful enough without pushing *Nancy* at her."

Everyone laughed nervously. But they were all looking at me.

"Why don't we let my aunt Clara decide if she wants to do it?" Plumy asked them. "Just because she can't speak, doesn't mean she doesn't have any brains."

She came over and knelt in front of me. "Clara," she asked softly, "would you take our daily allotment of fabric to the dyeing room at the end of the day? You could leave a note with it for Nancy, reading, 'I can't speak, but I'd very much like to meet you.' "

The silence in the room was terrifying. All eyes were on me, waiting. I felt Harriot's hand on my arm. "We need more names on our petition," she murmured softly. "If we got Nancy and her girls, it could bring in a *hundred* others."

Tears came to my eyes. I was so tired, my head was spinning. Across the room Elinora smiled at me and shrugged her shoulders.

"We won't tell anyone you did it," Plumy said.

I am the only one who can *do it*, I thought. By the time Great-grandfather finds out about it, I'll have my letter and money from Grandmother. I won't need my job. Why does the old man deserve my loyalty? And I'd get to meet Nancy before I left Lowell. Even if I couldn't tell her who I was, for fear word would somehow leak out to Nicholas.

Then I heard Grandmother's voice. *You must make your mark on the world. You must help others.*

Harriot got up to fetch paper and pen. I took it and smiled and wrote my answer.

Yes, I wrote.

Chapter Fourteen

At breakfast none of the girls in Plumy's circle spoke of the meeting last night. They mingled with the other girls and listened to how Professor Fowler had practiced his phrenology at their improvement circle.

"He measures peoples' skulls and does character readings from the findings," Moria told us. "He measured mine."

"And?" Plumy asked, "what did he find?"

"That I lack veneration."

Plumy scowled. "For what?"

"He didn't say. But now I'm anxious. Do you think that's why I laugh at Mr. Schell, our overseer, all the time?"

"No," Plumy answered. "I think you laugh at him because he's a silly fool to begin with."

The others began to make sport and guess what they would lack if Professor Fowler measured their skulls.

"I would lack humility," Clemmie said.

"He would just find that your head is too big," Plumy teased. Everyone laughed.

Plumy admitted then, good-naturedly, that likely she lacked patience. Harriot admitted to lacking humor. Everyone laughed as the game went around the table. Lucy Larcom said she lacked time.

Then it was Lizzy's turn. "I lack health," she said.

That put a pall on things. And it was time to go to work, so we put on our cloaks and went out into the February cold.

Not until I was walking along briskly with the others did I realize that I'd awoken with such a sense of anticipation at meeting Nancy today that getting up and dressing in the dark and cold had not bothered me at all.

I'd even eaten the mush they called breakfast.

Moria was tending three looms again. I felt a surge of dread as I stood at mine. Every day that I did not master the loom it frightened me more.

Moria pushed a metal lever and my loom started. Then, of a sudden, something went flying in front of me. In an instant, I ducked. In that same instant Moria shoved me aside and pushed back the lever that stopped my loom.

"The shuttle!" she yelled. "It's loose! The shuttle must be secured here, by the trough, on your right. If it flies free like that it could kill you."

I watched as she secured it. Then she started

my loom again. And, working three of hers, she managed somehow to keep an eye on mine all morning.

I wondered why Moria was not in the circle of girls who were pushing for the ten-hour movement. She worked harder than any of them. But she had a single-mindedness that made me think she had her own purpose for working in the mill.

I had learned by now that there were two kinds of girls in the factories, those who worked because they *had* to earn a living and those who came to Lowell because they wanted independence. Or to get out of their far-flung New England villages, to a place where there were libraries, lectures, and social and literary clubs.

Before I knew what was happening, Moria was by my side. "Watch the temple hooks!" And she was reaching over me adjusting the hooks, which were made of iron. In the next instant she replaced an empty bobbin with a full one.

"Sorry," I said.

I'd committed a grave sin. I'd been thinking. You couldn't indulge in thought when you ran a loom. You must become part of the machinery, like a shuttle or a temple hook. I knew I could never become part of the machinery. I was too much my own person.

Still, somehow I managed a little better that day. And though the aches I'd gone to bed with last night were now reawakened, I bit my lip and kept at it. The moments of the morning dragged on, each one drummed into eternity in my head. Tears came to my eyes. My throat seemed filled with cotton.

When I got back to the boardinghouse at noon, Emma called me into a small room that she used as an office. "You must sign this paper," she said.

"What is it?"

"A regulation paper. It requires you to attend some place of public worship every Sabbath."

I signed it.

She smiled at me. "What church do you attend at home?"

"Episcopal."

"You might do better as a Congregationalist here. It's what Mr. Chelmsford is. Always has been."

I nodded. "I don't care overmuch about church."

"Aren't you religious? I thought all you Southerners were."

How could I explain to her that at home, church was more a social affair than anything? "Daddy went to church to hear the sermons and keep up with the news and gossip. But of late he got tired of Reverend McElheran's sermons and started dropping in at the Baptist church."

My voice cracked, speaking of Daddy. "All our negroes go to the Baptist church. Christian slaves are worth more on the market than heathen ones."

"I must say you are forthright about slavery."

"I know you Northerners are against it," I said. There was no way I could explain our way of life to her. I would not try.

"How are you faring in the mill?"

"Not too good," I admitted.

"It will get easier. Since you see no wrong in slavery, I shouldn't have to caution you not to get involved in any of the anti-slavery meetings around here. No matter what Plumy or Elinora ask you to do."

My eyes widened. "They go to anti-slavery meetings?"

"When they have the time. There are quite a lot of anti-slavery people around. It marks one as a troublemaker if you join them."

"I thought all Northerners were anti-slavery."

She got up from her chair. "And where will the owners of the mills get their cotton if the anti-slavery people have their way? Whites won't work in the fields. And if there is no more cotton, tens of thousands of Northern mill workers will lose their jobs. Have you ever thought of that?"

We went into the dining room to join the other girls. No, I hadn't thought of it. I never had to. Now I did.

Before darkness fell outside the factory windows that day, Mr. Schell called me to him. Moria nodded that she would watch my loom.

He yelled in my ear. "You're to take the cloth to the print works today."

I nodded yes. And he pointed to a far end of the room where two girls had wound some freshly woven cloth so it wouldn't unravel. Every weaving room brought a bolt of freshly made fabric to the print works every day so Nancy could experiment with it for her designs.

"Can you carry it?" Mr. Schell asked.

I nodded yes.

"The print works is downstairs and across the yard," one of the girls yelled as she walked me to the door. "You can't miss it. It has a blue door."

I nodded. She opened the door for me. Moria came running over with my cloak and helped me into it. "It'll be closing time after you deliver this, so just go right on home."

The stairwell was empty. Strange to be the only one about. All around me machinery thudded. I had all I could do to keep myself from falling down the stairs.

Outside, darkening clouds threatened snow. The yard was dismal and deserted except for some men at the far end, loading finished bolts of cloth on to railroad cars.

I stood studying the building across the way. There were many doors. One read *Counting House*, another *Agent's Office*. Still another read *Storeroom*.

And then I saw it. The blue door.

It was the same blue as the doors of the negro cabins at home that kept away hants. And the same as on Great-grandfather's house.

I felt a strange sensation. The last thing Grandmother had said to me was that blue was my lucky color, and I should take comfort from it. Had she had a revelation?

I felt like I was having one now. I knew I belonged here at this moment. The knowledge was more than a feeling, it was part of my bones, part of the blood in my veins.

I had come here for this. I felt a sense of rightness. What had happened to me had not been an accident. It had a purpose. It was like the sun had just come out from behind the dark clouds and touched my face.

Was I the broken end of one piece of warp, sent here to be tied to the other broken end? So the fabric of my family, ruined for so many years, could be mended?

I started to cross the yard, walking toward the print works, clutching my bolt of cloth. Cold wind whipped at my cloak. Was I getting fancy notions, thinking I was coming home here in this filthy, unfriendly factory yard? How could it be?

Exhausted, I dropped the cloth just outside the door and stood staring at it. A brass sign above it read *Print Works*. Below was another sign. *Private. Keep out.*

Minding what I'd been told by Plumy, I knocked once. Loud. And waited. Nothing happened, but I'd been told nothing would happen. I was to knock again and wait.

The other girls who took turns doing this chore

every day would then yell "Cloth!" and leave. Of course, I couldn't.

So I did as I was instructed. I reached into my pocket for the piece of paper. On it I'd written what Plumy had directed.

My name is Clara. I am from the weaving room. I cannot speak. But I would very much like to meet with you.

In my pocket, also, was a copy of Plumy's ten-hour petition. Just in case the door opened, I pinned my note to the cloth. Then, of a sudden, bells started to ring and the great shuddering sound of machinery came to a screeching halt.

I looked up at the hulking buildings. The girls were coming, sounding like a wave about to break around me.

I ran for the gate. This night I would be home first. Since there were no assigned seats in the dining room, maybe I could get a chair next to the fire.

Chapter Fifteen

Though I had signed the paper saying I would attend church on Sunday, I did not go. Neither did Elinora. The reason was simple.

If we went out, Nicholas might find us.

This Sunday, when all the girls went to church, Elinora went back to bed. I took my tea into the best parlor to enjoy the peace and quiet.

Plumy wandered in. She had stayed home from church, too, pleading a headache.

"Wouldn't you like to walk out with me?"

All the mill girls walked out of a Sunday. It was considered an honor for a new girl to have someone ask her.

"I would love to, but I really shouldn't," I said.

"Nonsense. Here." She ran into the hall for some cloaks and came back holding a bonnet out to me. "Wear this. We call them our 'log cabins.' All the mill girls wear them. You'll be taken for one of us. No one will recognize you."

I looked at it. It was lovely and I didn't have

one because I had no money to buy anything. I hesitated.

"Come on," she said, "there's a February thaw. The sun will do you good. We don't see it all week."

She was right. Outside the sky was a flawless blue, birds were singing. "What are you thinking?" she asked me as we walked down Merrimack Street.

"Of home."

"Tell me about it."

I sighed. "Well, by now, even if Daddy is still unable to work, he'll have the negroes breaking the top crust of the land and hoeing under the old vegetation. He might even have them planting some rows of green peas and lettuce seed. Rob Roy, our overseer, will have old Hyder pulling the plow."

"It sounds nice. Like a different world."

"It is," I said.

We came to the canopied boardwalk that ran in front of the many fancy shops on Merrimack. Behind the windows were luscious displays, clothing, shoes, shawls, books, ribbons, gloves, games, bonnets, everything to tempt the mill girl into spending her hard-earned money.

"Look at that lovely dress," Plumy pointed to one in a shop window. Indeed it was lovely. White muslin with a blue sash. "Who wears such things?" she asked.

I shrugged. I'd been admiring some soft, white

kid shoes sitting next to the dress in the window. They were the kind Eessa May would like.

"Have you read the petition?" Plumy asked.

"No."

"Then let me explain about it. It's directed against the Boston Associates. Your great-grandfather is one of them. Girls have been working thirteen hours a day for the last twenty years in these mills, Amanda. Many of them have to leave each spring because they have the coughing sickness. Like Lizzy. She'll never be well. And she knows it. It's what makes her so ornery sometimes."

"What about the tonic?"

"It won't help. It never does. Eventually girls like Lizzy go home to die. And Moria. You see the way she blinks all the time? Well that's a nervous habit. She's the sole support of her mother and three sisters. They cut our wages a while back because no matter what happens, even if the price of fabric drops, the stockholders must have their profits."

She cast me a sidelong glance. "That's why Moria runs three looms at once. To make up for cut wages. They used to pay our board, too, but they changed that. Now we pay it out of our grand two or three dollars a week. You'll see. A dollar twenty-five a week will come out of your first pay."

I nodded, thinking. Was this why she'd asked me to walk? To bring me around to her way of thinking?

"Money means nothing to you, does it?" she asked.

I supposed she was right. "I never had any. I mean, Daddy always provided everything. But the reason I came North is because cotton prices were lower than ever and he and Grandmother wanted to get a higher price for their cotton. He needs money. To repair the house, to marry off my sister, and to send my little brothers to school on the mainland."

"Harriot is working to send a brother to Harvard. Did you know that?"

"No."

"We all have our secrets. Almost all the girls are sending money home. Some support widowed mothers. Lucy Larcom does. Her father was a sea captain who died when she was a child. She started in the mills as a doffer when she was eleven. When she was thirteen she started writing wonderful verses. She's been published. You know how she writes?"

"How?"

"In stolen moments while in the cloth room. Between cutting finished cloth and recording the number of finished pieces and bales. She's so tired when she comes home at night, but sometimes she stays up half the night writing, too."

She sighed. "All these girls would benefit from an hour or two more of leisure time in their day. Or a day off to go to a funeral. Do you know whose job you took in the weaving room?"

"No."

"Elvira Wentworth's. She was fifteen. Her dress got caught in the wheels of the machinery. She was pulled in. Before anyone could turn it off, she was mangled and killed."

We had stopped on the street. I know I had a stricken look on my face.

"I'm sorry to be so blunt. But Elvira was working three looms, too. And she was tired. It happens sometimes. They wouldn't even give us a day off to go to her funeral. Have I upset you?"

"I'm all right."

She nodded in approval. "Last year British textile workers won their fight for a sixty-nine hour week with six holidays. Our week was extended to seventy-eight hours, with only four holidays. Oh, Amanda, I'm sorry to do this to you, but we need you. We need your support."

We commenced walking. "You have it," I said. "But I won't be here long. I've written to my grandmother and she should be sending money for my trip home soon. But until then, you have it."

"Why?" she asked of a sudden. "Why would someone like you be willing to help us?"

I thought for a moment. "Grandmother told me to help others when I could," I said simply.

"But you come from a grand plantation. Your people are of consequence."

I laughed. "Not so grand. I told you my daddy needs money to repair the house. The truth of it is, my shoulders ache, Plumy." I turned to her.

"And my feet, too, even as we're walking now. And my fingers are swollen. That's why. I'm just like the rest of you. And I don't like it."

She hugged me. Right there on the street. "You *are* one of us," she said.

My eyes filled with tears. I felt proud. We walked for a while in silence then.

"The mill owners and agents should send their wives and daughters to spend a week in the factory," Plumy said. "They won't even allow them to visit. But it's just as well. We have too many visitors as it is. They bring people through to gape at us as if we're specimens. Senators come. Newspaper editors come. Preachers come. Editors of women's periodicals come. And many times you'll see a woman skulking behind her loom, hiding, when her husband, from whom she's run away, comes looking for her."

"Do you think Nicholas will come?" I asked.

"Yes. Sooner or later. But don't be anxious. We protect one another. Mr. Schell always tells us when a visitor is expected and who that person is."

I breathed a sigh of relief.

She started talking about the mill girls again, and how they had produced more than a million yards of cotton cloth last week.

"And women can never be overseers," she chatted, "though many of the operatives know more than the men who oversee them."

We walked along in silence for a while. "So now you know why the petition is so important to us," she said.

I said yes, I knew. I told her again I would help. And we continued with our walk.

A week later I received my first wages.

Two whole dollars!

I looked at the money in my hand. Never before had I earned money. Mine! I had worked for it, ached for it. I hurt from the earning of it. And now, for all my pain and tears, I had money in my hands.

How many times at home I'd heard Daddy talk about money. Or lack of it. Worry about "giving out." All Grandmother's trouble with Lillienfield came from arguments over money.

Never before had I understood any of this.

Now I did. Now I had some money of my own, that I'd earned. I felt a queer sensation. Pride.

I wanted to hoard it all and not part with any of it. And I wanted to spend it, all at the same time.

Of course, I had to pay my board out of it. But still. I would save some for a new calico dress for Sunday, I decided. I now borrowed one from Harriot, who wore the same size.

I would put a bit in the bank, in the Lowell Institution for Savings, where all the mill girls earned interest from their money.

And then I remembered. I wouldn't need to do any of this. Soon Grandmother would be sending money.

I felt another queer sensation. Could it possibly be *disappointment*? That I wouldn't be here to do any of these things? Was that possible?

Chapter Sixteen

Two weeks went by and I still did not hear from Grandmother. What was wrong? I worried the matter. There was a hollow space where my soul should have been every day when Emma handed out the mail just before supper.

Then I would comfort myself. The mail service was dismal, Daddy had always said. Or Grandmother had left Baltimore and my letter had to be forwarded to her at home.

She would write soon.

In those two weeks I still did not master the loom. I was starting to be able to tie the warp knots so they could barely be seen. But I still could not countenance the mind-sickening numbness from standing at the loom for hours.

Still, in spite of my disappointments, every day I felt myself drawn closer to the girls I lived with. Though I did not speak, I listened to their problems, became entrenched in their concerns. And they included me in all their discussions.

Several times I found myself pulling back from

some offered friendship. *I mustn't become too close,* I told myself. It will only make it more difficult to leave them.

I'd already had enough painful leave-takings to last a lifetime.

Every day, just before the closing bells, I would bring the bolt of fabric across the dingy mill yard and set it in front of the blue door of the print works.

Every day I would knock once, then twice, then wait for the door to open.

And every day nothing happened. So I would pin the same note to the cloth and leave it.

Near the end of February there was great excitement in our house. Clementine's letter was published in the *New York Tribune*.

Emma had copies of the newspaper. And there it was, every word Clementine had written right here on the desk in the best room, every word brought to life in print.

In spite of the fact that these girls published their literary poems and articles in the *Operatives Magazine* and the *Lowell Offering* regularly, this was different.

This was a New York newspaper.

It caused a great commotion in Lowell. People knocked on Emma's door and wanted to meet the esteemed Clementine Averill. That first evening the best room was crowded with visitors and Clementine received them all. She sat surrounded by Emma's girls, her eyes bright, her face flushed, receiving her visitors.

One visitor was a delivery boy. He came bearing flowers. "For Miss Clementine Averill," he said with a great sense of importance.

The other visitors were Mr. Schell and his wife, and Mr. Bruckland, the agent for our mill, and his wife and daughter. Mr. Schell was beaming. One of *his* girls had defended the Lowell factory system in a New York newspaper. Mr. Bruckland was so puffed up you would think he'd written the article himself. He'd sent over his own housemaids with platters of cold meat and cheese and relishes, dishes of iced cakes and pies.

Emma scurried about, serving coffee.

They all stepped aside when the ragged delivery boy handed Clementine the flowers. He was given a coin and left.

"Oh!" Clementine was greatly taken with the bouquet. "It's from Mr. Chelmsford! It says, 'To a flower in the City of Spindles.' And he's invited me to the first entertainment he has at his home after they finish their period of mourning."

Harriot, who was standing beside me, explained how, two or three times a year, Mr. Chelmsford put on an entertainment for selected operatives and employees.

"When is the period of mourning over?" Lucy Larcom asked.

"Whenever he says it is. He sets the rules," Harriot said. "True it was a great-granddaughter, but one he never met."

I felt the urge to laugh.

"You have brought honor to our mill," Mr. Schell told Clemmie.

I saw Plumy biting her lip. Did only I know what she was thinking? Who needs honor? We need ten hours.

"But I never did it for recognition," Clemmie said.

"No mind," Mr. Schell told her, "you deserve it."

After the visitors left, I stacked cups and saucers on a tray, helping Emma.

"You'll go, of course," Plumy was advising Clementine. "We must stay on his good side. And catch him off guard with our petition."

"Don't make me go alone," Clementine begged. "Someone must come with me. He'd have Nicholas down on me like a shot."

"Not I," Elinora said.

"Who then?" Clementine whispered.

"Mama," Plumy said. "She runs this house. She shall be your chaperone. It will put her back in his good graces."

"Me?" Emma looked surprised, but we could see she was pleased. "And what would I say to the man?"

"What he expects you to say," Plumy told her, "that you keep an orderly house. That your girls are all in the best of health, clean, industrious, moral, and availing themselves of all the culture Lowell has to offer. It's what the old coot wants to hear."

For a moment I had the wild notion they might ask me to go along, too. He was my great-grandfather, after all. And it would be the perfect way for me to get into his house and make him confront me.

But it was just that, a wild notion. Nicholas was still out there, waiting.

The next morning, as Moria and the other girls were about to pull the levers to start the looms, Mr. Schell called us around him. "We will have a visitor today," he said.

There were audible groans.

"No, no newspaper editors or senators or foreign visitors. Although I expect we'll be having an influx of them after that letter in the *Tribune*. This is a man looking for his wife and sister-in-law. He came to my office last night. It seems they ran away from him."

Snickers from some of the girls. A gasp from me. Nicholas!

Mr. Schell held up his hand. "You know I always give you fair warning about visitors. I'll say no more. If anyone here wishes to be excused when our visitor arrives, please let me know now."

Silence. I could feel my heart pounding. Nicholas must not find me here! I must ask to be excused. I didn't know what the girls knew about Elinora, but likely they were sensible of all the gossip. I would only be acting in character, as Clara.

I raised my hand.

Mr. Schell asked no questions. Bless the man. I couldn't figure out why the girls mocked him so. "Very well, Clara, when he comes I'll send you on an errand," he said. Then he gave the signal for the looms to start.

For once I was glad for the noise. Several times I caught some of the girls casting sidelong glances at me. But no questions were asked.

It was the way of them. They protected each other.

Still, all morning I was so nervous that twice Moria had to step in and tie my warp knots. My hands were shaking.

"Are you all right?" she yelled in my ear.

I assured her I was.

About an hour before the noon bells, a boy came to Mr. Schell and yelled something at him. Mr. Schell signaled to me. I waved to Moria and she smiled and nodded. My heart was pounding. My knees were weak. I prayed Elinora's overseer was as understanding if Nicholas came to her room.

Mr. Schell took me to the doors, where the noise was less deafening. "To keep me an honest man," he shouted, "why don't you take your bolt of cloth over to the print works now instead of later? Take your time. At least half an hour."

I understood and nodded. Our visitor was on the way up. Quickly I went to get my cloak, then walked over to the small pile of bolts that had been finished this morning. They were already neatly tied. I selected a bolt and struggled to the doors with it. I felt the eyes of the girls following me.

Mr. Schell opened the doors for me. "Hurry," he said.

I near fell down the steps, hurrying. Downstairs I opened the doors of the building carefully and peered out into the yard. It was, as ever, dingy and empty.

I pulled the hood of my cloak well over my head, so it concealed part of my face. Then I made my way across the yard to the print works.

The note for Nancy was in my pocket. I penned it every morning before I left for the factory. With it was my copy of the ten-hour petition.

I set the bolt down in front of the blue door of the print works. I knocked.

All I could think of was where I would go and hide after I left the cloth. Then behind me, I heard voices across the yard. Carefully, I turned.

Nicholas and another man were just going into the doors of the mill.

I turned back again to the blue door. I knocked again. I leaned against it.

Of a sudden, it opened.

I fell forward, with the bolt of cloth, into the arms of a woman. She was wearing a dark blue calico with white collar and cuffs. I saw that, and a gold pendant watch and ear knobs, and dark hair pulled back in a chignon, all in a blur as I tumbled in.

She grabbed me by my forearms or I would have fallen.

Her laugh was deep and real. "Well, so you're finally in, are you, girl? And the only reason is because I didn't know it was you knocking. You're early today." Her voice was rich and musical.

And so it was that Nicholas got me through the blue door.

Chapter Seventeen

She took the bolt of fabric and set it down. We stood in a small foyer. She locked the door, then turned and put her hands on her hips. "Now what's so important that you had to come knocking at my door every day leaving notes?"

I stared at her. She had high cheekbones and dark eyes. There was a warm, burnished cast to her skin. She was not white. Then I heard Grandmother's voice. *She was sent back home years ago, after Thankful died. She didn't have an easy time of it. She's half-Indian, you know.*

The woman in front of me wore silver scissors on a piece of rawhide around her waist. Her hands were long and slender.

"I don't have all day, girl. I was doing my weekly output report."

I shook my head and put my fingers to my mouth.

"Oh yes. You can't speak. A mute. Well," and she sighed. "I'm going against all my rules, but anybody as persistent as you must have something worth saying. Come into my office."

We went through a door to a square, neat room. Here was a small fireplace, a desk with a whale oil lamp, books and, on a bare wall, a large quilt.

A *quilt*. Yes! Another part of Grandmother's quilt!

I stood stock-still staring at it. It was of Indian design, dark reds, blues, browns. It had bits of fur, what looked like deerskin, ermine. I knew a wild turkey feather when I saw it and it had that, too. Besides some beads and fringe.

But one piece of it was exactly like a piece of fabric that had been in Grandmother's quilt. Red it was. Silk.

I felt a fresh stab of remorse at losing Grandmother's quilt. This was another part of it, after all. I felt dizzy, like you do when the past reaches out and puts a hand on your heart. I reached out to touch the quilt.

"Don't!"

I drew my hand back.

"It's old and fragile." Her dark eyes were filled with yellow flecks. She came around from her desk. "Do I know you, girl?"

I shook my head no.

"Do you know me?"

I bit my lip and shook no again.

She seemed disbelieving. "You remind me of somebody. That hair, those eyes. You're not in here to spy, are you? We get all kinds of people skulking around, trying to find out what our next fabric design will be."

I shook my head no again.

"Well, just in case you are, look all you want at the quilt. All the designs in it have been used already. Just don't touch." And she laughed again, deep and throaty, and set down pen and paper. "And when you're finished looking, write who you are."

I pretended to be gazing more at the quilt. But I was thinking. Should I tell her who I am? No, I decided. I was not sure of her yet. I must still protect myself. And Elinora.

So I wrote my name. Clara Clay.

She scowled. "Clay. Any relation to Emma who runs the boardinghouse?"

I held my breath and wrote. *Sister.*

"Ummm," she said. But she was still suspicious. "Clara, is it? I saw you once or twice when you were small. The Clara I recollect wasn't mute."

I wrote. *Riverboat accident. I've been South for the last year and a half. I was coming home.*

"Of course. Mr. Chelmsford's great-grand-daughter was lost on that boat. He's greatly upset. So, why have you been banging on my door?"

I took the petition out of my pocket and handed it to her.

She read it. The only sound in the room was the crackling of the fire. "Ten hours, is it?" she asked finally.

I nodded yes.

Her eyes went even darker with troubled intensity. "I've heard about the ten-hour movement. Can't say it isn't due. But it's going to cause trouble. I'm no stranger to trouble. But I don't trust papers. I never did."

I felt perplexed.

"It goes back to my childhood when treaties were never honored by the Shemanese." She smiled. "That's the Americans. I'm half-Shawnee. I suppose you've heard."

I nodded yes.

"My people would have had a council of war to decide about something like this. Let me tell you, girl, this will cause war with Mr. Chelmsford."

I nodded solemnly.

"My signature would get my girls to sign, of course. And then others would follow. There is strength in numbers. The great chief Tecumseh taught me that years ago. But still, why should I sign it?"

For your girls, I wrote.

She sighed deeply. "Yes, I suppose I should. But Mr. Chelmsford is not happy with me these days. Because I haven't been able to come up with a new design for our calico. I've been worrying the matter like a dog with a bone. For years now I've been able to keep turning out brilliant calicos with original designs. Now it seems I've run dry."

I listened.

"I told him I've been doing this too long. I want to go West, to teach Indian children. He says, 'Just make me one more design.' But I can't seem to conjure one."

I got a funny feeling on the back of my neck then. And a thought gripped me with such clarity, that had I chosen to speak, likely I wouldn't be able to.

I had lost Grandmother's quilt. But never would I forget the bird design in the center of it.

It had that bird drawing. On Grandfather Nate's letter. In his Bible.

It was a revelation, nothing less. And it filled me with a wellspring of hope.

I wrote. *I may have a design for you.*

"You?" She laughed. "Where would a slip of a girl like you get a design?"

I wrote again. *From the South.*

Now I saw the yellow flecks in her eyes again. "Where in the South?"

Baltimore, I wrote. The lie would have to do for now.

"Why would you give it to me?"

I looked at her steadfastly. And once again I sensed I'd been sent here for a reason.

The day I first saw her blue door I hadn't known the reason. This day I did.

It was to help the mill girls. "You will have power someday, Amanda," Grandmother had told me, "I saw it in my tarot cards. Promise me you will help others when you have the chance."

I wrote again. *For your signature on the petition. To help the girls.*

She sat down in her chair and eyed me. "You remind me of someone," she said again. "It will come to me. You are clever. But that's all right. One must be clever to survive in this world. Very well, Clara Clay, very well, bring me your design. We'll see what it looks like. Bring it by tomorrow, when you bring the cloth. And if it's good, I'll sign your petition."

I got up. The meeting was over.

"Maybe you were sent to me for a reason. I'm glad I gave you room to spread your blanket in here." She laughed. "It's an old Shawnee saying. They've made a proper New England lady out of me, but once in a while only an old Shawnee saying will do. Goodbye now. I'll see you tomorrow."

Chapter Eighteen

On the way back to the mill after our noon meal, Elinora rushed up beside me and pulled me away from view. "Did he come to the weaving room?"

"Yes. Mr. Schell sent me on an errand. What about you?"

"He came looking for me, too. Mr. Randolph, our overseer, let me hide behind some machinery. Oh, Amanda, I'm so frightened. Suppose he comes back? I'll have to go back with him. Because I have no rights. But he could kill *you.*"

"He won't dare try," I told her.

"And what makes you so sure, then? The man is desperate."

I wasn't sure. "I have friends here now," I said.

I didn't tell her. I didn't even admit it to myself. But I meant Nancy.

I hadn't told the others yet of the progress I'd made with Nancy. I wanted to get that petititon signed first.

That night I went to bed early, before the others. Alone in the room, I took Grandfather Nate's Bible out of the oilskin pouch. Inside was the folded-up, worn letter. I studied the sketch of the bird. Would Nancy like it? Would she cut out its shape and make a design for her new run of calico?

Think of it. A run of calico with a bird drawn by Grandfather Nate on it. The man my great-grandfather had disowned his daughter for. It was fitting, wasn't it?

I fell asleep happy. With the Bible next to me. Grandmother's quilt wouldn't be lost to the world after all.

I trembled as I handed the folded-up letter to Nancy the next afternoon.

Her brown eyes sought mine as she reached out her long, slender hands to accept it. She gestured that I should sit down.

"What is this?" She gazed at the bird sketch. I saw her eyes widen, saw her draw in her breath, study on it a minute, then she looked at me and smiled.

"What kind of a bird is this?" she asked. The same as I'd asked Grandmother.

I wrote on my paper. *Nobody knows.*

She nodded slowly and her eyes narrowed. She was thinking. Then, of a sudden, she opened a drawer and took out a large piece of paper and picked up a quill pen and began sketching. For a while all I heard was the scratching of the pen and the crackling of the fire.

In a few moments she was finished. Then she lifted the scissors she wore around her waist and began cutting out the bird she'd drawn.

My heart was beating very fast.

She cut and cut, smiling all the time. Then she showed it to me.

I nodded happily.

"I see it as white. In the middle of a field of blue. Like the sky."

Tears came to my eyes. It had been that way on Grandmother's quilt.

"Let me have that petition, girl," she said.

I pulled it from my pocket. With a flourish she signed her name. "I'd like to show it to my girls," she said.

Once again I felt that if it had been all right for me to speak, I would not have been able to. But I did have a question. Quickly, I wrote it down.

Won't Mr. Chelmsford be angry with you for signing?

She smiled. "Yes. And he will summon me. And he will rant and rave. And then I will show him this new design. And tell him it came from one of his hard-working operatives."

I shook my head, waving the thought away. Hastily I scribbled. *No. I do not wish him to know it was me.*

Again her eyes narrowed. "You're hiding something, aren't you?" she asked.

I kept my face straight.

"Any of the operatives would consider themselves fortunate to be signaled out by a mill owner for coming up with a new calico design. He'll reward you."

I shook my head no again. Then wrote, *Tell him to reward all of us with ten hours.*

She sighed. "All right. But I don't like people hiding things from me. You are closing up the path between us with briars. I would rather there was trust between us. Not for me so much as for you. I sense you have a heavy burden inside. And you need someone to talk to. Am I right?"

I gave her no sign that she was.

"You aren't Clara, are you?"

I bowed my head.

"Very well, I won't push you anymore. Just tell me one thing. Is this design stolen?"

I shook my head no vigorously.

"Where did you get it?"

I wrote. *From my grandmother.*

"But who that grandmother is, you won't tell me."

I stared at her stone-faced.

"Very well. I shall take the petition to my girls. You may come for it in two days. You, no one else."

Thank you, I wrote.

"Thank you. But I just wish you'd confide in me. Please know you have a friend here if you need one. I will honor your secret. I still have enough Shawnee in me to do that."

Chapter Nineteen

"Would you like to see the artwork for the bird design?" Nancy smiled across her desk two days later as she handed me the signed petition.

I could not see very much at the moment for the tears brimming in my eyes. I had walked around for the last two days, near bursting inside with the desire to tell the other girls of my accomplishment.

I looked at the petition.

Every one of Nancy's girls had signed it. All twenty-two of them. And Nancy's name was at the top of the list.

"I don't show my artwork to everybody, you know. Only special people."

I nodded yes, and she reached into a drawer of her desk and took out a small canvas.

On it was Grandfather Nate's bird. It was inside a circle of blue. The same blue as the door of the print works.

The same blue as the doors on our negro cabins at home. I just stared at it.

Nancy pulled a bell cord and a door opened. A young woman dressed in dark blue with white collar, cuffs, and apron, like hers, came into the room, bearing a tray of tea and cakes.

"I'd take you inside to the dyeing and print-rooms, but it isn't allowed. My girls all live in one boardinghouse. They don't mix with the other mill girls. We must keep our print room secrets. My girls even dress differently from you."

I nodded. *Thank them for signing,* I wrote.

"When will it be presented to him?"

Not until we get many more names. But we'll get them now.

"Well, it will undo him." She sighed. "And this is a man who is more accustomed to undoing others. Do you know how he got the land for this mill?"

I shook my head no.

She poured tea. "He needed water power for his new mill. So he set out to buy land on the banks of the Merrimack River. He told the farmers he wanted to raise fruit and wool. So they sold the greatest water power in New England for near nothing."

She handed me my tea. "When they found out his real reason, and the money they could have made, they were very angry. But could do nothing. So they made a song about it. And schoolchildren sing it today."

She stirred her tea, recollecting. "His very grand house stands near the river and he did keep part of his promise. The garden is a wonder, with fruit and flowers of such perfection. And the wool, well, people still laugh. He kept that part of his promise, too. He pulled it over their eyes."

She smiled at me and I felt some sense of companionship between us. I smiled back.

"By the time they give him the petition, my new calico run should be ready. That should restore his soul."

I had not set out to restore the soul of this great-grandfather who had cheated the farmers. Or turned me out.

"What is it you want to know from me, child?" she asked.

I raised my eyebrows. I was getting very good at that.

"Come now. I know there is something burning in you. What is it you wish to know?"

Why does this place have a blue door?

"No one has ever thought to ask. Mr. Chelmsford's granddaughter, Mrs. Ebie, did that. A cousin came up from the South years ago and told her about the blue doors they have down there to keep away hants. You know what hants are?"

Without thinking, I wrote. *Ghosts.*

"Well, Mrs. Ebie was greatly taken with this cousin. His name was Jemmy. I met him, too. It was during the war. Jemmy was killed shortly afterward on the *Constitution*. Mrs. Ebie visited his home down there once. And met Eliza Pinckney, who kept growing indigo after the other planters stopped because the market here collapsed. She was exporting it all over the world. Mrs. Ebie had some sent home. It made our first, good color in calico. And our doors blue."

My tea was getting cold, listening to her. My heart was beating very fast.

"Well," she went on, "that indigo blue print was lively and pretty. It had a small white spot sprinkled all over it. It wore like deerhide and it made Mr. Chelmsford's mill famous. But *before* that, you know what our first color print was?"

I shook my head no.

"Red. That was back in '23. It cost two and threepence, which is about thirty-seven-and-a-half cents a yard. It was a bad color." She chuckled. "I'd dyed fabric before. In the old mill. Using the old ways. But Mr. Chelmsford, he was pushing to use new methods."

She shook her head, remembering. "I told him, 'pokeberry boiled with alum for red,' but no, he would have his cowhides. Well, it had a white spot in the middle of it. Mrs. Ebie had a gown made of this fabric. He promised people it wouldn't fade. Well, it didn't do *that*, but the white spots washed out, leaving holes. Mrs. Ebie laughed. 'I always was more holy than righteous,' she said to me."

Her face grew somber then, and she held her teacup in two hands in front of her and stared into it. "What else is it you want to know, child?"

I shivered. She was *clairvoyant.* Like Grandmother!

Tell me more about Mrs. Ebie. Grandmother had told me next to nothing.

"Well, let's see. Oh yes. She married her childhood love, Benjamin Cleveland. He's a merchant. He's turned his vessels to bringing in raw cotton for the mills. And he exports our textiles. They have one son, studying in Europe. They're visiting him now."

So then, I had a cousin. Grandmother had been thoughtless not to tell me. But had I ever asked?

"Only three of the old man's children gave him issue." She chose her words carefully. "Abigail, Thankful, and Cabot. But why am I telling you this? You aren't interested, are you?"

I nodded yes.

She eyed me narrowly. "Well, Cabot's daughter is Mrs. Ebie. Only one of Abigail's children had children. The girl they sent North was one. But she died, of course. Never have I seen such a family for bad medicine as this one."

She sipped her tea. "The old man wrote to Abigail's lawyer to send another grandchild. But the lawyer wrote that they can't come." She sighed. "Poor Abigail."

Then Grandmother *had* received mail from up North before I wrote! But her *lawyer* had written back. Why? Oh, I minded, Great-grandfather doesn't correspond with Grandmother. Still, if his mail got there, why not mine? And why *poor Abigail?*

Nancy spoke quietly. "And I'm a granddaughter, you know. My mother was Thankful."

I smiled.

"Yes, but it isn't the same as the others, being that I'm half-Shawnee. We get on, but it never will be the same. And I never married. My girls here are my children."

I said nothing. The fire spit. Silence for a moment.

"That first blue print with the white design in it? You know what that white was?"

I shook my head no.

"It was from Star Watcher's dress. She'd gotten the cloth from an Indian agent."

Who was Star Watcher?

Her voice got husky. "Sister to Tecumseh, the great Shawnee chief. People who hated Indians were walking around in dresses made like that of Star Watcher's. My grandfather hated Indians because they took my mother. And the print made him even richer."

And now, I thought, he will love this new print. And it was drawn by Grandfather Nate, whom he hated, too.

I felt the ending of things. And the beginning. As if a circle were being drawn around me. Like around Grandfather Nate's bird.

"Well, I certainly have gone on," Nancy said. "Told you more than you wanted to know."

I leaned forward to write. *Yes. But the blue inside the circle of the new design is the same as the blue on the doors.*

She nodded. "You are taken with those doors, child." And she shook her head. "I like the blue, that's all. That color has always been good medicine for me." She laughed. "As you see, I still use some Shawnee expressions. My grandfather doesn't approve. But I told him once a long time ago that I would always be Shawnee in my heart."

She stood up. "Here, let me give you back your paper with the bird on it. You'll want to keep it."

I took it and thanked her.

She smiled. "I couldn't help reading the letter that sketch was on the back of. Somebody was in the Canaries, all sick and fighting the British. Who could that be?"

I blushed and lowered my gaze.

"Well, I must get back to work. Come see me again sometime. Maybe you'll want to tell me if that man who was in the Canaries ever got home. And if not, come anyway. The council fire between us burns nicely."

Chapter Twenty

I had the petition.

I stood outside the blue door of the print works, not believing it. *I had the ten-hour petition, signed by Nancy and her girls.*

Now others would follow. There would be more signatures. Maybe hundreds. I looked around me at the tall brick mill buildings, the wide mill yard.

I had done this! Without me it wouldn't have happened. I had traded off Grandfather Nate's bird, drawn in the cabin of a ship years ago off the Canary Islands, for these signatures.

The man who was in the Canaries finally got home.

More than that, Grandmother's quilt, stolen by Nicholas, would come alive again in the new calico print.

I felt a surge of peace. As if Grandfather Nate himself stood next to me. In this mill yard owned by Nathaniel Chelmsford who had always hated him.

I drew the petition from my pocket, unfolded it, and stared at it.

We the undersigned, it read. And there were the names: *Nancy Chelmsford*, bold as brass, was the first one. Under it were others. Strange names, mill girl names. New England names. Not Daphne or Eessa May. But *Serephina* and *Leafy*, *Florilla* and *Aseneth*. Names like *Ruhamah*, *Almaretta*, *Algardy*.

I felt good, as if I'd done something of note. It made all the pain in my shoulders and feet and hands worth it. *Grandmother*, I thought, *you said I would have power someday to help others. Well, I've done it.*

And besides, I thought to myself, *I've found Nancy.*

In the confusion of the boardinghouse hallway, with the girls coming in from the cold, taking off their cloaks and bonnets and talking about their day, I handed the petition to Plumy.

She read it and screamed. "Oh, we've got it!"

Everyone stared at her.

"We've *got* it!" And she ran into the dining room, where some girls were already seated, grabbed a spindle-backed chair and stood on it, as she must have stood on that pump a few years ago.

"Girls, listen. Please, this is very important. The ten-hour petition we've been working on has been signed by Nancy of the print works! And all her girls!"

She held it up for them to see.

I heard some girls gasp. "They'll be dismissed," someone whispered.

"Good for them," another said.

Emma came in from the kitchen bearing a tureen of soup. "Plumy, get off that chair. Whatever are you up to now?"

"The ten-hour petition. We got Nancy and her girls to sign it. And she's signed it, Nancy *Chelmsford*. Imagine that!"

"Well, and how else should she sign it?" Emma set the tureen down. "That's her name. Now come, girls, have your soup before it gets cold. Plumy, get off that *chair*. You can just as well discuss this at the table like a civilized human being."

"All right, Mama. I just want to say one more thing to everyone. We wouldn't have had these signatures if not for Clara."

Everyone applauded. I ducked my head and sipped my soup.

"She *talked* to you?" Lizzy asked. "She would never even answer the door for me. However did you do it?"

I blushed and shook my head.

"I won't push those of you who haven't signed yet." Plumy spoke to the girls not in her circle. "But I think you needn't be so fearful of signing our petition now."

Afterward, as the girls filed out of the dining room, to go out to lectures or take sewing into the best room, Elinora lingered at the other end of the table.

"I must tell you. Nicholas has secured a position as gardener at Mr. Chelmsford's house."

"A gardener?"

"Yes. Spring is coming. It's March. He's a good hand with gardens. At home he kept a beautiful one."

"At my great-grandfather's house?"

"Yes. Emma was doing her marketing today. And a friend told her."

"But how can that be?" I whispered. "Don't you recollect how the lawyer there told us they didn't like Nicholas?"

She smiled at me and I noticed the dark circles under her eyes and the thinness of her face. She didn't look well. This fear of Nicholas had really eaten away at her. "One thing about Nicholas. He can be very charming," she said. "He can win anyone over with charm if he tries. And he grows beautiful roses."

Fear struck at me then. And all the happiness of my afternoon was washed away.

"He knows we're here in Lowell, Amanda. And he isn't leaving. But I am."

"You?" What was she talking about? What was she saying?

"Yes. I've spoken with Emma about it. And she agrees it's best. I can't stay here anymore. I can't wait for him to find me."

"But where will you go?"

"To my father. In Princeton. I have a father in Princeton. Didn't Clara tell you of him?"

Truly now, I was unable to speak.

She gave a deep sigh. "I've written to him. He has written back and invited me to stay in his home with him. His housekeeper recently left, you see, and I can keep house for him."

"But," I said hoarsely.

"But what?"

"Nothing." I shook my head. *But you stayed with Nicholas when you should have left,* I thought. *And because of that, he hurt Clara. He made her like stained Sea Isle cotton. He tagged her and ruined her forever. Her fear of him made her change clothing with me. And so she is dead. And here I am now, in the mill. And you can leave. And I can't.*

"Your father abandoned all of you. And now you're going to him?" I said.

She smiled wanly. "Yes. Oh, Emma isn't happy with me. She won't have anything to do with him. But he's old now, Amanda. And not well. I can help him. And he can help me. Don't be angry with me. You aren't, are you?"

I thought, *Poor Elinora. Running from one man who harmed her to another who'd done the same.*

But it was none of my affair if she was so weak that she kept delivering herself up to men who had done her wrong, was it?

Oh, I didn't know. Where I came from we couldn't live without our menfolk, either. We needed their protection. They had all the power, as Grandmother had said. But she'd also said it was different in the North.

Apparently it wasn't. Nicholas had as much claim on Elinora as Lillienfield had on Grandmother. Oh, I was so confused. And tired of it all.

"No, I'm not angry with you," I said. "I wish you well." And I started from the room.

"Amanda," she said, and she was beside me. "I hope you won't try again with your great-grandfather after I leave."

"No. Why should I do that? I have my pride, Elinora. I know when I'm not wanted."

If the barb hurt her she never let on. "You don't know what a despicable man Nicholas is. He'll stop at nothing. You don't know what he can do."

"I do know," I said levelly. "I know what he did to Clara."

It was like throwing cold water in her face. She pulled back. Then she gathered herself in and nodded. "Then you know why you mustn't go there. Promise me. I wouldn't leave if I thought you were in danger."

I nodded yes.

"Wait for your grandmother to write," she said. "I'm sure she will. Please promise me you'll wait and leave Lowell when she writes."

I promised that, too. And left the room.

That night I wrote another letter to Grandmother.

Chapter Twenty-one

March 1841

Elinora packed her bags and left two days later. And within the week it was as if she had never been in the house at all.

"They'll forget about her," Plumy said of the other girls. "It's always that way when a girl leaves. The world swallows her up and they stop thinking of her. Another one comes to take her place."

"That's because most of them wish they could leave, too," Emma said.

"And because our girls usually go on to a better place," Plumy added.

The air was heavy with meaning. Was it better where Elinora was going? Neither Emma nor Plumy would speculate. And nobody did speak of Elinora after she left, not even Emma. Well, I would remember her, always. After all, she changed my life.

In the next two weeks all you heard about in Lowell was the ten-hour petition. But you heard about it in whispers. They were like the undertow on St. Helena's Island, when the tide flows back to the sea. Soft, but with a treacherous strength.

Spring came to Lowell. Not like it came at home. Here the sun would be blessedly warm in the morning and by afternoon the March wind would gather all the cold left in New England and rush it down our streets.

No letters came from Grandmother.

Sometimes I was so enmeshed in the goings-on at the boardinghouse and the mill, that I almost forgot Grandmother. She and home seemed like another lifetime. Like something lived by some other girl, not me.

Certainly not by the girl who wore the sturdy shoes that she was only now able to lace up because her feet were no longer swollen. Or the girl who was getting as nimble as Moria with the loom. And certainly not the girl who was earning her own money and had just bought a new calico dress that my sister Eessa May wouldn't have worn to a hog killing.

Why hadn't Grandmother written? The question plagued me, stalked me on Lowell's wind-torn streets.

Had my letters been lost? Had Nicholas contacted my family and done his evil work, warning them someone pretending to be me would write?

Or was Grandmother still trying to teach me to be strong? What a cruel joke, if that were the case.

Grandmother, I'd whisper to myself, *if this is another one of your lessons, I will never forgive you.*

It was part of my regular duties to bring the bolt of fabric to the print works every day. And I looked forward to it. The thought of Nancy, with her cup of tea waiting for me, her yellow-speckled eyes, her slender hands and her warm laugh, telling me stories of the mill, made it possible for me to get through the long toiling hours each day.

"Come, spread your blanket," she'd say. Then she'd tell me things.

"I'm over forty now. No longer young. I've been working for Mr. Chelmsford since I was your age. I want to go West and teach the Choctaw Indian children."

Or: "My mother was taken by Indians when she was your age. She had one blue eye and one green one. They called her *Much Favored.*"

She would stitch on something while she talked and sipped tea. I would just sit and let the aches in my shoulders and legs melt away.

It wasn't long before I realized that she was stitching something other than her needlework in those sessions.

She was stitching together a picture of the family for me. Deliberately and bit by bit. In the same way she had made her quilt.

I was fascinated by the family. And in her wise way, she knew that. Yet she did it in a way that made it seem it was my questions that led her on.

You said Mr. Chelmsford had another son. Law-rence. What happened to him?

"He and his wife, Mattie, took a trip West ten years ago. They got as far as Chicago. And ran into an epidemic of Asiatic fever and died."

Had Grandmother known this? I felt anger growing in me for all she had not told me.

What about Mr. Chelmsford's other daughter? You said her name was Hannah.

"She married a man named Richard Lander. He brought the first shipment of pepper into this country when he was young. I loved him. He was always good to me. He officered his *Black Prince* on a voyage one day in '26. Uncle Cabot, Mrs. Ebie's father, went with him. One day out there was an awful October gale. It made widows and orphans all up and down the coast."

I shivered. The March wind blew against the windows.

"Aunt Hannah died soon afterward. This is a star-crossed family," she said, setting down her needlework and picking up her cup of tea. "Which is perhaps why I always held myself a little apart from them."

A star-crossed family indeed. It was fitting that she, a half-Shawnee Indian, should be the one to tell me about them. She with her Indian sayings, the gold of a lost people in her eyes. She, who for all her accomplishments, would slip back into the ways of her people in an instant if she could. That is the way she struck me.

— *212* —

One day she told me about the Pawtucket Indians who used to gather in this place called Lowell. "Every spring, they came, to catch the running salmon," she said. "Likely they camped right where the mill stands now."

What happened to them?

"What happens to any of us?" And she laughed, that musical laugh of hers that sounded more and more to me each day like the wind. But not any wind I'd ever heard. Some other wind, I thought, in some other place, far away.

That night home was all I could think of as I left Nancy's and walked to the boardinghouse.

The potatoes would be planted already. By the tenth of March Rob Roy would have planted the yellow yams. Also the water and muskmelons and March corn. Did they ever speak of me?

Emma's house was in a state of high excitement when I walked in the front door. All the girls were at supper already. I slipped into an empty chair next to Lucy Larcom.

"Did you hear?" she asked. "Isaac T. Hopper wrote a letter in reply to Clemmie's in the *Tribune*. Not only the *Tribune* ran it. He sent another copy to the *Boston Daily Times*!"

I lifted the small piece of slate Mr. Schell had given me to wear around my waist. And took some chalk from my pocket. *Who is Isaac T. Hopper?*

"Only one of the most famous Quaker philanthropists," Lucy told me. "He said the mill girls wouldn't suffer by comparison to daughters of Southern slaveholders."

"It means," Plumy said from the end of our table, "that Mr. Chelmsford must be in heaven right now. Listen to this." And she read from the paper.

" 'I experienced so much gratification reading thy letter that I could not resist the inclination to tell thee how pleased I am with it. Senator Clemens's original remark, saying the life of the Southern slaves is better than that of the mill girls, shows to what extent Southerners will defend slavery. It also shows the ignorance of the Southern people as to the condition of the Northern operatives. Some years ago I attended a meeting in Lowell at which were present about three hundred factory girls. I was so pleased to observe their happy countenances, modest behavior, and deportment. I saw no gloom or despondency. And I think they would not suffer by a comparison to the daughters of Southern slaveholders. . . .' "

Plumy's voice trailed off. Then she folded up the newspaper and fanned her face with it. "Eliza," she said in a mock Southern accent, "get me my lemonade. Now. I have had the most *fearful* morning overseeing those wretched slaves in the kitchen. I'm exhausted."

Everyone laughed.

I didn't.

Then Plumy's voice got angry. "If a renowned Quaker says such about us, who will think our petition has any substance? And we've got almost a thousand names on it! How can our plight matter to that old goat in his mansion now? Or to the *Boston Associates* who own all these mills?"

No one spoke for a minute. Then Clementine did. "I didn't know my letter would cause such trouble, Plumy. I'm sorry I ever wrote it."

"Oh, don't be silly," Plumy said angrily, "nobody blames you. The point is, we want this petition to go before a special committee of the Massachusetts Legislature eventually. What will our legislators think after reading this?"

"That we're a bunch of complainers," Harriot said, "unless . . ." Her voice trailed off.

"Unless what?" Plumy pushed.

"Unless someone responds to Hopper's letter and tells of our true plight. And how we *would* suffer by a comparison to the daughters of Southern slaveholders," Harriot finished.

"Who would be able to respond?" It was Moria, from a table across the room. All the girls were listening now, not only the girls in Plumy's group.

"Who would be able to say what it feels like to be the daughter of a Southern slaveholder?" Moria said again.

"We could go to the library and study about it," Harriot suggested.

Several of the girls murmured their approval.

"It wouldn't work." Emma spoke up for the first time then from her table near the window. "It would have to be written by someone who knew.

And who could compare your lot with rich girls in the South." She did not look at me when she said that.

"What will we do, then?" Harriot asked.

"Eat, everybody," Emma told them. "You need your nourishment. You can think on it and have a meeting after supper. But for now, eat. I won't have my food go untouched."

They commenced eating. Conversations were picked up. A buzz of talking filled the room.

I picked at my food. My heart was beating very fast. I did not look up from my plate as I ate my mutton and squash. Because I knew that when I did I would see Plumy's star-brown eyes fastened upon me. And I knew there was something else this girl would expect from me now.

Chapter Twenty-two

They had a meeting in the best room after supper. I pleaded a headache and went to the dreary little room on the third floor. The beds were neatly made and the girls' meager personal possessions were placed neatly in the bandboxes with which they had arrived in Lowell. On each was sewed a card with her name on it.

I had no bandbox. I had no portmanteau. I had nothing. I'd come to Lowell wearing someone else's clothes and bearing someone else's name.

I felt a sudden sense of desolation sitting there on my tiny bed, as I had not felt since I arrived here.

I was worse off now than Elinora, who at least had a father to keep house for. I didn't even know if my own daddy was still alive. As for Grandmother, well, I might as well just get the idea of her right out of my head.

Did anybody care about me? Downstairs the girls were having another of their everlasting meetings. They had them at the drop of a hat. They were going on like a passel of fools over a stupid letter written by a stupid Quaker man that they thought would ruin their stupid petition.

I was sick to the teeth of their petition. Hadn't I done everything I could for them? Well, I knew one thing. I wasn't going to do any more.

And when Plumy came through that door, as I expected she would any minute now, and asked me to write to the newspaper and say that mill girls *would* suffer by comparison to the daughters of Southern slaveholders, well, I just would refuse to do it, that's all.

I'd done enough. For everybody. I just wanted to lie down here on my bed and rest. And forget about the whole world. And when I woke up I wanted to be in my bedroom at Yamassee. And look out the window and see Daddy riding off to hunt on Black Hawk, calling to his hounds, who would be yelping and baying and running after him.

Oh, I wish I had some of Daddy's blue pills!

It was after dark when I felt the hand on my shoulder and heard Plumy's soft voice. I opened my eyes. She had a lamp in her hand.

"The meeting's over. We have to talk, Amanda, before the others come up."

I'd been dreaming about old Hyder. That he had the distemper and was dying. "I'm not doing it. Don't ask me, Plumy."

She set the lamp down on a small table. It cast

her shadow against the wall, larger than life. "You're the only one who can do it."

"Haven't I done enough? I got Nancy and her girls to sign the petition." The bad taste of the dream was in my mouth. I started to shiver and cry.

"What's wrong? Are you ailing?"

"I had a bad dream."

Emma appeared in the doorway. "I've brought a tray of tea. And some cornbread." She set it down and hovered. "Plumy, have you made her cry?"

"She had a bad dream, Mama."

Emma felt my forehead. "No fever. What's wrong, child?"

"I dreamed that old Hyder was dying. He's our best plow horse. And now I mind that he was sick when I left. And I don't know whether he lived or not."

"Sometimes the messages in dreams need to be studied on. I'm sure he's alive. Plumy, don't push her."

"Yes, Mama."

Emma left the room. Plumy handed me my tea. I sipped it. The dream cleared from my mouth and my head. "I miss home so much, I want to die."

"So do all the girls here."

"But they get letters."

"Many of them are homesick. It's the least of their problems."

"Can't somebody else write the letter?"

"There is no one else."

"It isn't fair."

"Most times things aren't. Haven't you learned that yet?"

"Nicholas is out there, waiting to *kill* me, Plumy."

"Do you think your great-grandfather would let that happen? Think."

"I'm tired of thinking. I want someone else to do it for me. I want my daddy."

"In heaven's name don't be a little Southern goose, always crying for her daddy. Do you see any of us doing that? We stand on our own feet."

"Well, I'm tired of it. My feet hurt."

She laughed. "Aren't you proud of your accomplishments? Look what you've done since you came here."

I admitted it begrudgingly. "Yes."

"Then here's one more you can be proud of. And this letter may be a Godsend to you. Here is a way you can tell your great-grandfather you're alive without going near the house."

"If I wanted to let him know I was here, I could have told Nancy. In a minute she'd go to him for me. I just can't take that chance. Nicholas is going to kill me."

She peered at me with her star-brown eyes. "Do you trust me, Amanda? Haven't we become friends?"

Again I had to admit it. Begrudgingly.

"Then believe what I say. Your great-grandfather is a powerful man. *He won't let that happen. You must trust in that, Amanda.*"

Trust? I looked at her as if she'd suddenly sprouted horns. "My grandmother doesn't write to me," I told her, "My daddy sent me away. My great-grandfather wouldn't even *see* me. How can I trust anybody?"

"Trust *me.*"

I pushed the thought aside. "I don't see the others putting themselves forth."

"Do you know how often I've put myself forth, Amanda?"

"You're different. You're strong. I'm not."

"Well, I wasn't always. I had to learn. And you can, too. I'll help you, Amanda. You have it in you to be strong."

"Some of the others wouldn't even sign the petition."

"Forget the petition. It's worthless if this letter doesn't get written. And only you can do it. Only you have the power."

I looked at her. In the eerie light cast by the whale oil lamp, I looked at her hard.

"Trust me, Amanda," she said again.

I wished, oh, how I wished, that she hadn't used that word, *power.*

Chapter Twenty-three

"You look tired," Nancy said the next day.

Tired was not the word for what I was. I was a broken thread in the loom. I had two ends, one down in St. Helena's Island and the other up here. And they couldn't be strung together.

I have bad dreams.

"Of what?"

I dreamed of Old Hyder, our plow horse. Twice. Only the second time, I saw my Grandmother's negro girl, Sabrena, in her red turban. She was crying for Hyder.

"You have been given a sign," she said.

Of what?

"Tell me first what you wish to see me about."

Who I am.

She held up her hands in a gesture of encouragement.

And so I told her. Everything. How I'd been sent North. How Grandmother had been so clair-voyant, how she'd told me I would have power someday and I must use it right. I told her about

meeting Elinora and Clara, Nicholas, the riverboat wreck, all of it.

All the while, she just listened and her face
never changed. When I finished she smiled.

"You're not surprised," I said.

"No."

"Why?"

"The bird. I'd seen it before. Years ago, your
grandmother wrote to my aunt Hannah and sent
her a sketch of it. I didn't recollect right off where
I'd seen it. And you mentioned the South. And
you were so interested in the family."

"When did you know?"

"The day I gave you the signed petition."

"You were playing with me then."

She smiled. "Come now. Weren't you playing
with me?"

Our eyes met and we laughed.

"And then you always reminded me of someone.
It wasn't until I recollected about the bird that I
knew who. My aunt Hannah. You look a lot like
her."

"Why didn't you say something to me?"

"You weren't ready to clear the path between
us. Now you are. But I do not know why this day
is any different from the others."

I told her about the letter Plumy wanted me to
write. "I don't know what to do. I thought you
could help me."

"You know what to do. You just need to hear
yourself say it to someone."

I was confused.

"And you said it to me just now. When you told me your grandmother said you would have power."

"But what about Nicholas? What if he harms me?"

She smiled. "You have me. Do you wish me to go to your great-grandfather now and open the path between you and him?"

"No," I said quickly. "Because I must write the letter. Then you can help me. But not to beg my case with him. I don't want him if he doesn't want me."

She smiled. "I said those words once about him, too."

"You can help me if I have trouble with Nicholas. Though I hope by the time the letter is published, Grandmother's lawyer will have written. I posted another letter to him this morning. I can't understand why *she* hasn't written to me."

A startled look came into her eyes. Then I saw the gold flecks. "You don't know then, Amanda?"

"Know what?" I felt myself slipping down into some hole inside me, some hole I'd known was there all along, that I'd been sidestepping without realizing it.

"I'm so sorry. I thought you knew."

I gripped the arms of my chair.

In the next moment she was standing over me. She put her arms around me. "Word came to us just a few days before you arrived here. She died.

That's what the black crepe on the door is for. Didn't you see it?"

I groped, trying to find something to grab onto as I fell in the hole.

All I could find was Nancy. I clung to her. "I thought it was for me," I wailed into her apron. "Everybody back at the house said it was for me."

"Everybody back at the house didn't know about your grandmother."

"Why didn't you tell me!"

"I didn't know who you were at first. And then I suspected. But I couldn't put out the council fire between us, by talking out of turn."

Grandmother dead! I couldn't fix it in my head. Always, she had been there for me. And here I'd been waiting for her to write! Oh! I felt myself falling again.

Nancy held me. "Your dreams were signs, Amanda. That's why you've been dreaming of the horse dying. And your grandmother's servant crying."

"Is my daddy all right? Has Great-grandfather heard?"

"Last they heard, he was mending."

But Grandmother! Dying before I'd even gotten here! And all the while, I'd thought she was alive! Oh, I felt so turned in on myself, so cheated.

All this while I'd been writing to and hoping to hear from a dead woman.

"I only wish I hadn't lost her quilt," I murmured.

"It may be returned to you. Mine was to me."

"Oh, if only it could be. I'll hold onto it forever!"

She gazed at hers on the wall. "If you want me to, I'll go over there and tell Mr. Chelmsford who you are. This very afternoon," she offered.

I gulped and wiped my tears. "No," I said, "no. I must write the letter. Grandmother would want me to."

I felt strong, saying it. *And why not,* I thought, going back out into the deserted mill yard. Plumy told me I could be strong, didn't she?

Chapter Twenty-four

"I'm sorry about your grandmother," Plumy said.

I bent my head over the desk in the best room. I could not bring myself to reply. "If I write this letter, I write in my way," I told her.

It was after supper that same night. Most of the girls were out and the doors of the best room were closed to the others. They'd just have to receive any callers in the second-best parlor.

"Your way?" She looked dumbfounded.

"Yes. I've been studying on it. I'm not angry like you are. Or self-righteous."

"What are you then?"

"I'm tired, Plumy. And I miss home. And I'm pure sad. And I can't use any of the fancy phrases these girls here use when they write. And I won't say any of the claptrap this Mr. Hopper wants to hear."

"Claptrap?"

"Yes. Claptrap. He won't experience gratification reading my letter. When I get done, Mr. Hopper will feel like he's standing fifty feet from the best Kentucky rifleman, right in the line of fire. Do you still want me to write it?"

She smiled. "Yes," she said. She went to the door, paused, and looked back at me. "Yes," she said again, "write it." And she left me there then, alone in the best room.

I started to write.

Oh, I introduced myself proper-like. Even a judge at a watermelon contest would do that.

I told him who my grandmother had been, who Daddy was.

I am the daughter of a Southern slaveholder who finds herself in the unhappy position of being stranded in the North, without funds, without recognition from family. I have had to earn money for the trip home by working in one of the mills.

Then I got right to it.

I could never live in the North, Mr. Hopper. You see, I just found out that my grandmother died. There is no time off when you are a mill girl, for grieving. Not unless you are willing to give up your wages. And I cannot do that.

Where I come from, when someone dies, neighbors gather around and bring food. Relatives come and stay for days, bringing their servants with them. And family intrigues drown out the sorrow, if seeing to the comfort of your guests doesn't.

Then, when everyone leaves, you have time to sit

and stare out at the sea grasses or the pasture land.
You take your strength from such things.

At home today, instead of slaving over the loom,
I'd be sitting on our back verandah, watching our negro
Rob Roy overseeing all hands as they bank the ground
for cotton. A smart shower might be threatening on
the horizon. I'd take strength from the potatoes sprout-
ing in the fields, or the pretty way the March corn is
coming up, from the wind blowing through the sea
grasses and the new colts in the pasture.

What is there to look out on here, if indeed, I had
the time? Dingy buildings? Row houses? Mill girls with
their pale faces bowed down as they hurry to work?
Where do people get their strength?

There is no time. Everyone is always hurrying. The
week before I arrived, the girl who worked my loom
before me was killed when her dress got caught in the
machinery and she was pulled in. She was fifteen. And
the girls who worked alongside her didn't even get time
to go to her funeral.

I told him about Lizzy Turner, who coughed so
bad she would soon have to go home to die. And
about Moria and how she had to work three looms
to make up for having her wages cut and as a result,
had a nervous habit.

When our negroes at home are sickly, my daddy
tends to them and gives them time off. When they die
we bury them proper-like. And everyone attends the
funeral.

Then I told him about Lucy Larcom, who stayed up nights writing her beautiful poetry because she had no other time to do it.

My friends here are as refined, intelligent, and agreeable as any I have had back home, Mr. Hopper. But that is where the comparison ends. No, they are not inferior to any class of women in the South. Except in the way they are made to work for their wages.

You say the slaveholders are guided by avarice. I write to tell you that the mill owners are, also. You quote John Wesley in your letter, saying "Slavery is the sum of all villanies."

I do not defend slavery. Nor do I wish to enter into a discourse about it with you. But you would be hard put to find a mill owner against it, as they could not run their mills and make their profits without Southern cotton.

And, as the daughter of a Southern slaveholder who has worked in the Northern factory, I write to tell you that Southern slaveholders are not the sole authors of such villanies, sir. They not only exist, they thrive here in Lowell, too.

Yours respectfully,
Amanda Videau

Chapter Twenty-five

April 1841

We not only had the petition circulating amongst the mill girls now, we also had a letter calculated to enrage my great-grandfather that might any day appear in New York and Boston newspapers.

I felt the ending of things. And the beginning. And neither one looked too promising to me.

It was April. And, as all through March, spring tried to come to Lowell, but could not quite manage it. One moment the sun would be warm, and the next the winds were back with all winter's force. Some mornings there was still ice underfoot.

You could not even trust the weather in Yankee land.

I went about my work, but I worried the outcome. "I care more about how the girls will feel about me than what my great-grandfather will say," I confided to Nancy a week after the letter had been sent. "They'll hate me for not being honest about who I am."

She laughed. "When I first came to Salem everybody hated me. Mr. Chelmsford made me sleep in the lean-to next to the kitchen. I know hatred, Amanda, and I wouldn't worry. Those girls are your friends."

Plumy was waiting for me on the front step, waving something. "Amanda, hurry! You've done it. Both the *New York Tribune* and the *Boston Daily Times* have published your letter!"

She had them in her hands. Both papers. "Amanda," she whispered before we went into the house, "I must tell you. I took this opportunity to strike while the iron was hot. This afternoon, our petition, with two thousand names on it, went to Mr. Chelmsford."

There is something about seeing your own words in print for the first time that is very frightening.

My words. My thoughts, my feelings, put down in neat newspaper columns for everyone to read and remark upon.

I felt exposed, naked, proud, unbelieving, and humble all at the same time. I had given away part of myself to the rest of the world. And yet it did not diminish me. For the first time in my life, I felt as if I really knew who I was.

The girls were very excited. They squealed and gathered around me.

"We knew you were different all the time," Moria said.

"I knew it from the first morning," Lizzy put in.

"It's all right," Plumy told me. "You can talk to us now."

I sat dazed at the table. They were all staring at me, not only Plumy's crowd at our table, but the other girls as well. There was no anger on their faces. Some were smiling.

Tears came to my eyes. "I'm sorry I had to deceive you all," I said.

There was a general outburst, remarks about my Southern accent, questions about my home. There was talk all around as platters of food were passed.

"Girls, let her eat." Emma came in with tea.

"Does your father really own slaves?" from Harriot.

"Are you terribly rich?" a girl named Agrippa asked.

"Tell us about your grandmother who died," from Clementine.

I picked at my food and answered their questions. But there was no anger from any of them. This alone brought a knot of tears in my throat.

"I want to know about the sea grasses," Lucy said dreamily.

Lizzy went into a fit of coughing. "I want to know what your daddy would give me for this," she said.

Then from Moria: "How does it feel to have spent your last day at the loom?"

"My last day?"

"I told you girls to wait until she got a decent meal in her." Emma came back with a plate of hot bread, set it down, and surveyed the lot of us. Then she sighed and pulled a letter from her pocket. "It's from Mr. Chelmsford," she said. "It came to me late this afternoon."

A buzz of excitement went through the room. "Read it!" the girls at the other table all said in unison. "Read it to us, Emma, please!"

She looked at me and I nodded. "Read it," I whispered.

So she did. To say that she did not feel important was to say that the mills were not run by water power in Lowell. But she was also very sad and mindful of her responsibility.

" 'My dear Mrs. Clay,' " she read. " 'It has come to my attention, through the most unusual means, that you have, as a boarder, a relative of mine. That her identity be revealed in the newspapers is a great shock to me. I have been receiving inquiries from all over town since her letter was published. One was even hand-delivered to me from Boston. And I dread to think of what the mails will bring.' "

The girls cheered.

" 'Through the most unusual means,' " Plumy mimicked.

"Hush, Plumy," her mother ordered. Then she continued. " 'I have assured all who are concerned that I was not aware of her presence in Lowell, but that she was in the best of hands, being in your house and your care.' "

At this all the girls in the room applauded.

When they finished, Emma went on. " 'My dear lady, this situation is most embarrassing. But such sentiments pale in comparison to the joy that followed at learning that my great-granddaughter, thought dead these months, is still alive.

" 'Please tender to her my felicitations and use every bit of your authority to see to it that she does not report to the mill another day. I shall expect her at my home at four in the afternoon, tomorrow, Thursday, April fourteenth.

" 'Again, please know you are in my debt for the care you have given my great-granddaughter, and that I will do all in my power to see you are properly recompensed. I am, with sincere regard, Nathaniel Chelmsford.' "

"Well?" Moria insisted, "how does it *feel?*"

But I was not given the chance to answer. For there was a general outburst from the girls in the room. And then, by the time Emma calmed them down, Plumy and Harriot, who had left the room, came back and were holding out a large package.

"This is for you, Amanda," Plumy said, "from all of us."

I felt dazed. "What is it?"

"We took up a collection," Harriot said. "You can't meet your great-grandfather in that old dress."

I could scarce untie the string. Plumy had to help me. When the brown paper was laid aside, I gasped in disbelief and delight.

There was a new dress, made of calico.

It was blue and white calico with a delicate lace collar and cuffs. The design was a bird.

Grandfather Nate's bird.

I burst into tears, then looked in dazed wonder at the smiling faces all around me.

"It came from the first run," Plumy explained. "We asked Nancy for it."

"We never knew the design came from *you* until she told us," Harriot put in.

"She told you?"

"Everything," Plumy said, "including how you offered your bird for our petition. Mama sent a note to her and she let us in. She really spoke to us! And helped us get a dressmaker to do it up, quick. Do you like it?"

Did I *like* it? "I can scarce speak," I said.

Everybody laughed.

"Girls, girls, no one's even finished eating yet," Emma scolded. "The food is getting cold. And I've got a special cake for dessert."

"We owe you a lot, Amanda," Plumy said.

I hugged her. "I'm the one who's beholden to you," I said. "I never knew I could be strong, until you showed me."

Tears were in my eyes. I released Plumy and looked at the others, into their faces which had become so dear to me. "I may not be a mill girl anymore," I told them, "but I wouldn't have missed knowing you all. Not for anything."

Chapter Twenty-six

"So, there you are! Come in, girl. Don't stand there like the town pump."

I jumped, startled. The voice was strong. It came from down inside him with roots that went deep. And I'd been jumpier than a cat with a long tail in a room full of rockers since Emma had left me at the front gate.

She'd walked me here. With instructions that I was to have my great-grandfather send me back in his carriage.

I'd promised and hurried inside.

My great-grandfather stood in the room Elinora and I had been received in last time. A maid was with him.

"Amanda, is it?"

"Yessir. Amanda Videau."

"Well, come in and sit down."

He shuffled, aided by the maid, to sit in a chair by the fire. He gestured, with his cane, that I should sit, too, and I did. The maid took my cloak.

"Will you have tea now, sir?" she asked.

"Eh? Yes, of course. And cake. You like cake, Amanda Videau?"

"Yessir."

He grunted and scowled. He was looking at my dress. Then he stared at me, at my face, my hair. "So you've come back," he said.

"Sir?"

"Come running back to me as I knew you would. What's the matter? Can't live with that Southerner you ran off with?"

I stared at him in horror. *He thought I was Grandmother.* Was the man taken with dementia, then? He was so old. His hair, what there was of it, was pure white and thinning so you saw through to his pink scalp on top.

His face was mottled with age spots. His hands trembled. He was well turned out as far as his clothing. But the rich cloth of his frock coat sat uneasily on his bony shoulders.

"What are you staring at, Amanda Videau?" In the next minute he was back in the present.

"Nothing, sir."

"I'm ninety-three. I fought in the Revolution."

"Yessir, I heard."

"They're all dead, all my children. Heard, did you? Did they tell you my privateer, the *Black Prince*, kept the Americans supplied when they had the British penned in Boston in '75?"

I nodded yes.

He gave me a grin. And I saw a death's head in front of me and shivered.

Just then the maid distracted him with the tea tray. She made a great show of setting it down. Then she started to pour and spilled some. "Begone with you, girl, and leave us be. Young Abigail here can pour for us. She always poured tea for me as a child. Didn't you, Abby, my girl?"

"Yessir," I said.

The maid left.

"Damned Irishers," he said. "All they're good for in the mills are scrubbers and waste-pickers. They're all over town, like flies. Catholics! Pour my tea."

I poured, handed the cup to him, and watched him take it with shaking hands. Somehow he managed not to scald himself. He slurped it loudly.

"Cake."

I cut him a slice and put it where he directed.

"So you don't like my town, hey?"

I sipped my own tea, not sure how to reply.

"Well? Own up to it! Did you write that letter in the papers or didn't you?"

"My name is on it," I said.

"Didn't ask you that, Amanda Videau. I asked, *did you write it.*"

"Yessir, I wrote it."

He slapped his knee. "Own up to it! Do you know what Charles Carroll said when he signed the Declaration of Independence?"

I shook my head, no.

" 'That's Charles Carroll of Carrollton, Maryland, if the king wants to know where to find me.'

Only worthwhile Catholic I ever knew. Do you stand behind your words?"

I set my teacup down. "Yessir, I do."

"You weren't influenced by the troublemakers in that house, were you?"

"Great-grandfather, those troublemakers are my friends. They took me in when no one else would. Everything I wrote is true. And I meant it."

He waved my words aside with his cake fork. "This whole town was my idea. Right from the beginning, from my first little cotton yarn mill in Beverly, I knew Americans could be independent of the British with their textiles. I started it years ago. And this town now, is known all over the *world*."

I listened.

"Yankee ingenuity! That's what did it. I teamed up with Sam Slater and Kirk Boot and others to start these mills. But the idea was always *mine*. Isn't that something to be proud of?"

"Yessir, but . . ."

"But nothing, young lady. Lowell is a model of industrialism. Our young women are the best. No child labor here. No paupers' graves, like they have in England. Profit, virtue, doing good and doing well, those are my bywords. So then, what have you to complain about?"

"The girls are overworked," I said. "They never see the sun all winter. Some have coughs. Lizzy Turner will likely have to go home to die this spring. Girls get killed and maimed in the machinery. They have to run three looms because wages were cut. The air is bad in the mills. The cotton flies about. They need better ventilation."

He sat back in his chair, holding his cane between his bony knees with both hands. He seemed sunken in on himself.

"You're a brazen little piece," he said. "If they're so overworked, why do they have time to write such cultured words for magazines? Why do they go to evening schools? Learn music, foreign languages, botany?"

"To keep themselves sane," I said. "The work breaks the back. But it breaks the mind more."

He glared at me. And I saw such hatred in his eyes that I wanted to shrivel up and die. "You would find a way to get back at me for trying to keep you from your Southerner, wouldn't you, Abigail?" he asked plaintively.

I shivered. The fire was dying in the grate. The day was turning gray and cold outside. *Oh God*, I thought, *now he thinks I'm Grandmother again. What's the profit in all this?*

"I always hoped you'd come back to me. You were my favorite. Not Thankful. And you ran off. I knew you would come back someday. But not like this!"

I wanted to cry. *He* was crying. I saw tears coming down his face. I did not know what to do.

"Great-grandfather," I said. I made a move toward him.

He waved me off with his cane. "Did you sign that petition, Amanda Videau?"

I sank back in my chair. He was back in the present again. "Yessir," I admitted.

"It will ruin me, ten hours. It will ruin all of us."

And then I had a thought.

"Great-grandfather, in England, the country you fought against for our independence, the mill workers have a sixty-nine hour week. With six holidays. Our week was extended to seventy-five hours. With only four holidays. Don't you think American girls deserve as good as the English?"

His face seemed to sharpen. And he looked like a fox to me suddenly, then, a fox about to pounce. "You're like that Southern grandfather of yours," he said to me. "I never trusted him. Ran off with my daughter, he did. And I don't trust you either. Why did you come here, anyway?"

"You asked me to. You invited me."

"I told you never to cross my doorway again, Abigail, if you marry that worthless slaveholder."

I stood up. My napkin and spoon fell to the floor. "You may say my grandmother married a slaveholder, but you couldn't run your mills without Southern cotton," I said.

His crying got worse.

It was a terrible sound. I became frightened and looked around for the maid.

"Sir, please, you mustn't excite yourself." It was the popinjay lawyer, J. Solomon Aldrich. He came rushing into the room. "What are you *doing* to him, young woman?"

"This is my great-granddaughter, Aldrich," Great-grandfather said. He looked up, wiping his eyes. "Isn't she something to see?"

"Ah, yessir. But you mustn't excite yourself."

"Who wouldn't be excited meeting a great-granddaughter for the first time? Looks like Hannah, doesn't she? Blood tells. It always tells. Oh, that's right, you didn't know Hannah. You missed something, Aldrich. They don't make them like Hannah anymore."

I felt grievous-bad. Surely, the old man was demented.

J. Solomon patted Great-grandfather's forehead and shook his own head. "He's perspiring. I'm afraid you must go. I'm sorry for your inconvenience, but it's as I thought. This has done him no good."

"But I just got here."

"You're exciting him. Do you want to kill him? Is that what you set out to do?"

This exchange was done in savage whispers. But the old man caught on. "You're not sending her away, Aldrich."

"Sir, you are too agitated. She can come back another time."

The old man smiled. "Another time, yes. We've had a lovely visit. And look, Aldrich, she's wearing the new print in her calico. Isn't it a beauty?"

Aldrich gave me a fleeting look. It was a dismissal, nothing less. "It's lovely," he said.

"Soon everyone will be wearing it," the old man told him. "And it comes from my mill. You look very fetching there, young lady. What is your name again?"

I stood and picked up my cloak. "Amanda Videau," I said.

J. Solomon Aldrich settled him. It took a few moments.

I was not sure how to say goodbye. But I knew I would not be back again. This was not working. "Goodbye, Great-grandfather," I said.

"Give her the envelope," he directed his lawyer.

"Yessir." The man walked me into the foyer. "This is a little something for all your trouble," he said. "It will get you back home and reimburse you." He held out an envelope.

"What's wrong with him?"

"He's old. He isn't well. We try to keep it secret. Mrs. Ebie and her husband run things. But for the sake of appearances, we allow people to think he does. I hope you will honor our secret."

"Where I come from we know about honor," I said.

"Mrs. Ebie would have welcomed you properly. Their ship is due back from England any day. I'm sorry you had to meet him like this. But that letter of yours in the newspapers. And that petition. Well, it's set him back terribly. Of course, we're glad you're alive and not dead." He started to say

more, then stopped, and was completely be-
wildered.

I could see he was one of those people Grandmother had spoken of, who thought silence was
an abyss he'd fall into.

"Did you write to my people and tell them someone was pretending to be me?" I asked.

"No." He held out the envelope again. "Please
take this. He wants you to have it."

I wondered if that was true. Or if J. Solomon
wanted me to have it. To go and not come back
again. Chances were, tomorrow, my great-grandfather would not even remember I'd been here.

What could I do? I needed the money to get
home. I could not work in the mill any longer. It
was a disgrace to the old man.

I took one last look at him and accepted the
envelope. "Thank you," I said.

He opened the front door. "A wind has come
up. I can have our gardener walk you home."

"No!"

He smiled at me, an ascetic, unused smile. "It's
a new gardener. The maid hired Mr. Rhordan
without our consent. We dismissed him. I'll get
the new gardener."

"No thank you," I said. "I'll be right fine." I
wouldn't ask this man for a carriage or a gardener.
I went out the blue door as I'd come in. On my
own.

Chapter Twenty-seven

A gust of wind caught the skirt of my blue and white calico and blew it up. My cloak billowed out behind as I went down the walk.

Wind was blowing dust, bits of old dried leaves, even sticks, upward in a spiral. An early and ominous darkness had gathered. Tree branches swayed and creaked with an otherworldly sound. I fancied I saw shapes as I opened the wrought-iron gate and stepped out into the street.

The wind had a cold bite to it. Lightning threatened on the horizon.

It was fixing to be a good New England storm. I hurried, head down. Up ahead I saw two carriages. The horses had their heads bent to the wind. I lowered my own head and hoped I'd make it home before the rain started.

Lamplight from inside houses seemed to blink at me. In a flash of lightning I looked up and saw that the two carriages were gone and I was alone on Merrimack Street.

My footsteps echoed as I hurried. I heard the

gasping of my own breath. And then I heard something else.

Footsteps behind me. Slow and measured, but keeping pace with my own.

I turned. It was a man.

I felt abandoned, alone in the world. And frightened. Oh, why hadn't I accepted that popinjay lawyer's offer to let the gardener see me home? Why hadn't I kept my promise to Emma and asked for their carriage? They owed me that much. I was family!

This was no night to be about alone.

I turned around once more, nearly tripped and righted myself. *The man was coming closer.*

Nicholas!

My heart was hammering. My breath was spent. I crossed the street. A branch crashed down from a tree, just missing me. I ran under the canopied walk of the stores and turned again.

He was getting closer. I felt fear, a bitter bile in my throat. Oh, the brass of him! He knew I was a great-granddaughter of the most powerful man in town! Yet he would harm me! Had he no sense?

No. He must harm me to save his own skin. I must always remember that.

It did not help now, though. What to do? All the stores were darkened, some shuttered already. I gathered my cloak around me and ran.

Behind me Nicholas ran, too.

Rain started coming down. First just a splattering, cold on my face, then great drops. I heard it pattering on roofs. Then it came with a vengeance, cold and slashing. It ran down my face, it blinded me. It mingled with my tears. Wind tore the breath from me, worse than any we had at home.

"Think you can get away from me, girl? I waited for you to come out!"

What should I do? Hide in an alley? No, I'd get past the shops and bang on the first house door I came to. If I could make it.

Oh God, I prayed, help me. Don't let him catch me. I don't want to die.

Fear is a terrible force. It is a dark, cold hand on the heart that renders you as good as dead. No! I was determined I would not give in to it. Anger gave me new determination and strength.

And then I saw it. Up ahead, a terrible distance away, but I *saw* it. A lantern. *Someone was coming.* Oh, someone was mercifully coming. If I could keep going until I reached the lantern carrier I knew I would be safe.

Behind me I heard Nicholas's labored breath, closer and closer, the stomping of his footsteps.

Closer and . . .

He reached for me, got hold of my cloak, and pulled. I screamed and pulled free.

". . . teach you a thing or two, you damned little Southern brat."

And I felt an ironclad arm around my neck, pulling me down. No, I mustn't fall. I mustn't!

We went down together, off the wooden walk, onto the sandy street, already puddle-filled. We both fell with a hard thud. I heard him groan, heard something crack, heard him yell in pain.

But his arm was locked around me and I couldn't free myself. I kicked. "Let me go!"

He was on his knees, then his feet, pulling me up. He had to yell to be heard in the howling wind. "Where is she? Where's my wife?"

"I don't know!" I yelled back.

He hit me full force on the face. The blow sent me into unconsciousness for a moment. Then I came to. He was shaking me again. The world was a dazzling array of lights, whirling rain, darkness, and then lights again. My eyes cleared and I saw distant lamps from houses where people were gathered, warm and secure against the storm.

Then everything went black and I felt myself fighting against wet wool. Around and around he turned me inside my blackness.

I screamed, but it was muffled.

He'd thrown a blanket over me!

"I'll let you go, Miss Sath Kalina," he said. "In the river."

He picked me up. I smelled whiskey and other vileness from him. *He was going to throw me in the river to drown.*

I kicked and screamed. But my arms were bound tight and my screams muffled. My heart felt about to burst. I wouldn't die like this, like some rat caught in a trap. I was going back to Emma's. I had money in my reticule, which I still clutched close to me.

I was going home.

But he carried me like a sack of potatoes for about another fifty yards while I kicked and screamed. Then he grunted and buckled and crumpled to the ground.

I rolled out of his grasp and into a cold puddle, struggling to get free. I was mindful of a scurrying nearby. I heard gasps and grunts. Then a final groan from Nicholas. And all went quiet except for the sound of the rain.

"Help me," I called out. "Please."

"Hold still, child. How can I untie this thing if you don't hold still?"

Nancy.

In two minutes she had the blanket off me. "Nancy, where did you come from?"

She pulled me to my feet. "No time to talk," she said. "I think I killed him with my scissors. Can you run?"

Chapter Twenty-eight

Four days later I stood with Nancy on the wooden platform of the train depot on Merrimack Street. It was mid-morning and spring had finally come to Lowell. The day was clear and mild, the sun warm, buds were in bloom. The long months of winter seemed like a dream to me.

I was going home.

I was traveling by train and stagecoach. Tickets were in my reticule, along with money, and a letter sent by Mr. Roux, Grandmother's lawyer.

My letters to Grandmother had been forwarded to him. But he and my family had received another, unsigned letter. From the North. Warning them that someone would be writing to them who was impersonating me. It must have come from Nicholas.

Mr. Roux had accidentally left his carrying case at my daddy's house one day. Ty and Garland had found my letters to Grandmother inside. And insisted the writing was mine.

The news had caused great turmoil in the house.

Rob Roy was painting the sulky and had to stop and help Daddy onto Black Hawk for the first time since he took sick. The dogs knocked over the paint, ran through it, and into the kitchen. Lavinia burned the supper and Eessa May cried and fainted. And Daphne said good I was alive, plans for Eessa's wedding were wearing her down, and she needed help.

Mr. Roux wrote that Daddy needed my moral support in his fight with Lillienfield, too. Was I up to it?

I was. Garbed in my blue and white calico with the bird on it, I was ready for anything. I had a new cloak and shoes, new underthings, a new portmanteau and bandbox, a ginger cake from Emma and the kisses and tears of all the girls.

I'd given some of the money from Great-grandfather to Moria, for minding my loom so often, and some to Lizzy Turner for a good doctor.

Nancy's horse stood waiting patiently, hitched to her wagon which was full of supplies. Nancy was going West, to teach the Choctaw Indian children.

"Seems the train is late." And she laughed. "Are you all right, Amanda?"

"I'm fine, Nancy." I was the only passenger waiting. The depot was deserted. An unsettling quiet lay about.

"You remember to take the medicine the doctor gave you for your head." And she laughed again. "I'll wager Nicholas hurts more than you do."

Nicholas was not dead. She had only wounded him with the scissors. The magistrates came to question me at Emma's house, where I'd stayed, recovering. I told them about the riverboat accident and Nicholas. He'd been turned over to the authorities.

I had not seen my great-grandfather since that night. The town newspaper had carried a story about how Nicholas attacked me. But no word came from Great-grandfather at all.

"Does the old man always act demented, Nancy?"

"No. He's quite good when Mrs. Ebie is around."

"Did he say anything about me when you said goodbye?"

"It was a hard goodbye. He's not very happy with me since I signed that petition. Or with you. You walked in there, bold as brass, and told him everything he was doing was wrong. I'm afraid he'll never forgive you."

"You didn't ask him to, did you?"

"No, child. I never did ask him for anything and I won't start now."

We sat down on a small bench. "Do you think the Englishwoman who's taking your place will do as good a job?"

"Yes. And she's promised to look after my girls. And already orders are coming in from everywhere. As far away as England!"

We smiled at one another. All over Lowell,

women were already buying the fabric sporting Grandfather Nate's bird.

"Do you think the petition will amount to anything?"

Nancy sighed. "No. Not yet. I think it will take a few more years for people to come to their senses. But I heard he's been taken to task by his business cronies in New York and Boston for allowing his own kin to work in the mill. I don't think they'll be living this down for a while."

The sun was warm and I leaned back on my bench and closed my eyes for a moment.

Then Nancy made a sound in her throat. "Oh, my."

Someone was coming toward the platform. A woman. A beautiful woman in a silk dress of blue and pink. She looked like all the wealthy ladies I'd seen walking on Merrimack Street, sleek, well-cared for, and expensive. She had a package in her hand.

"Who is it?" I asked.

"Oh, my," Nancy said again. And she stood up.

The woman came up the steps and toward us. She and Nancy fell into each other's arms.

"When did you get back?" Nancy asked.

"Last evening. And I heard everything. Oh, to think I almost missed you! And you're leaving! When?"

"Today."

"Why?"

"It's time," Nancy said.

The woman accepted that. "I shall miss you. Thank God you were here to do what you did the other night. I didn't believe it when I heard the child was turned away. It's, why, the whole thing is uncanny! It's what happened to you, all over again."

"I know," Nancy said.

I just sat staring.

Then the beautiful woman turned her gaze at me. "And this is Amanda then?"

"This is Amanda," Nancy said. "Amanda, this is Mrs. Ebie."

I jumped to my feet. "Oh."

"My dear!" She reached for me. She drew me into her arms, crushed me against her silken bosom. I smelled lovely perfume. She was beautiful. There was a sweetness about her that made you know nothing bad ever happened to this woman. She was not young, no. Why she must be in her forties! But I'd known women like her at home. In twenty years she'd still have that youthful sweetness.

"Look at you," she said, "Aunt Abigail's granddaughter. You're a lovely young lady. Oh!" And she held me at arm's length. "Jemmy's niece. Oh, I knew your uncle Jemmy, child." Tears came to her eyes. "This family has lost so much. And yet, I look at you and I see Jemmy. Yes, I do. And Aunt Hannah."

I'm all that, I thought? And then I thought, *Where were you? If only you'd been here.* But she

— 255 —

hugged me again and I scarce could breathe.

"They didn't tell me until this morning that you were leaving. I ran almost all the way. Oh, child, I am so sorry for what happened to you. And so put out with Grandfather. He allows Mr. Aldrich to influence him so!"

"It's all right, ma'am," I said.

"No, it isn't. Working in the mill! Shameful! Benjamin, my husband, and I try to tell him he must make improvements, like they've done in England. But he won't listen!" She shook her head. "But I can't believe it. Why, you suffered the same fate as Nancy when she first came here." She looked at a small gold watch that was attached to her dress. "How long before the train arrives?"

"It's late," Nancy said. "We have time. They're always late."

"Not enough time, I'm afraid. Listen to me, Amanda. Don't go away hating us, please."

"I don't hate you, ma'am."

"I shall come to visit you. Would you like that?"

"Yes." I meant it. I would.

"And I have something for you." Ebie handed the package to me.

I tore off the paper. Something fell out.

Grandmother's quilt.

"The magistrates delivered it to the house early this day. That dreadful man still had it," she said.

My quilt! I hugged it close. "Oh, I thought I'd lost it." I held it up. "You see the bird in the middle?"

"I see," Nancy said.

"Thank you, Mrs. Ebie, thank you."

Then we saw them coming. The woman pushing a man in a chair with wheels. She pushed him up on the siding. They came toward us. I recognized the Irish maid.

He was wearing a woolen cloak and a tall beaver hat. He took off the hat as the girl stopped the chair. He motioned her away. "See you beat me here, Ebie," he said.

"Yes, Grandfather."

"Gave her the quilt, did you?"

"I did."

"Last time you gave a piece back to Nancy. And she gave it to me."

"On the deck of the *Black Prince*," she said, "at Aunt Hannah's wedding."

He nodded. "Take the quilt home, Amanda. Repair it," he said.

"My grandmother wanted it here. She said it should be pieced together with the rest of the quilt."

"Good idea," he said. "You come back and visit. And do the piecing. Nancy?" He looked at her. "You want to leave your part? Or do you have to take it West, to the Indians?"

Nancy smiled. "I could leave it. And I could come back for a visit, too, if I was invited. And help Amanda do the piecing."

"You're invited," he said.

Nancy nodded her proud head. "I'll fetch it

now," she said. And she walked to her wagon.

"And I'll help too," Ebie said. "I've got Aunt Hannah's piece. We'll work on it together when you come back, Amanda. Just like Aunt Hannah, Aunt Abigail, and Aunt Thankful would have done."

"My grandmother would have liked that," I said.

Great-grandfather took out his handkerchief and blew his nose. "We read about you in the paper. Didn't your grandmother ever tell you that a lady only has her name in the paper when she's born, when she marries, and when she dies?"

"Yessir, but I never was much of a lady," I said.

"Neither was my Abby. Hung her drawers out the window of the widow's walk to send a signal to your grandfather. See you're wearing that dress again. Very clever of you to offer your design. Fresh it is. Different. Would you say it's the only good thing my son-in-law ever did for me?"

I was about to answer no. But Nancy did. She had come back to the platform with her piece of the quilt and handed it to Ebie. "No," she said. "From what Aunt Hannah told me, Nate Videau did a lot of good. He was a fine man."

"Can't say," the old man muttered. "Didn't know him. Sometimes people fool us. I wasn't fooled by that gardener, though. Knew he was up to no good. To think if it wasn't for Nancy here, you could have been killed. I owe you a debt, Nancy."

"No matter," she said. "Anyone would have done it."

"I am in your debt, nevertheless." He looked again at me. "I'm not daft, you know. Just get a little forgetful at times. I'm better now that Ebie is home. I have my senses about me still. Enough to know Aldrich is wrong when he said you near ruined us in the papers. I told him, maybe we ought to pay you some mind. That it's a sorry day when Englishwomen have it better in the mills than American women. Is that what I fought for in the war, I asked him!"

In the distance, we heard a train whistle.

He put his hand inside his coat pocket and drew out a paper. "I wanted to give you something."

"You've given me money already," I said.

"This isn't money. It's an order for more cotton. Give it to your father."

I felt a lump in my throat as I took the envelope.

"Thank you. I'm sure Daddy will be most gratified, sir. It will help."

"Never liked your damn Sea Isle cotton. Too coarse. But we'll give it a try. And you tell him I want all white, no stained." He shook a finger at me.

"It won't be stained," I said.

Again the train whistle sounded, this time closer.

Again he drew something out of his pocket. With shaking hands he opened another paper.

"This petition," he said. "This is trouble. You know that, don't you, girl?"

"Yessir," I said.

"I was never one to be afraid of trouble. And I can't make you any promises. But I'll bring it up in my next meeting with the Boston Associates."

I felt a thrill. "Thank you, Great-grandfather." I leaned over to kiss him. His face was like wrinkled old paper.

"They've been berating me. How could I let my great-granddaughter work in the mill? Told them, if it isn't good enough for her it mustn't be good enough for anybody. And maybe we ought to permit some inquiries."

Nancy had walked back to the bench to get my things. The train was chugging into the station, clanging and shrieking. It ground to a stop.

Nancy came over with my things. "Time to board," she said.

I looked at her. Then at Mrs. Ebie, then at the old man. There were all kinds of things I wanted to say, things I knew I never could say. I leaned toward him again.

He waved me off. "Go on with you. And a more proper way you go, than your grandmother went, out the window."

I laughed. But I was crying. I hugged Nancy. Then Mrs. Ebie. I walked to the cars.

"Goodbye, Abigail."

I turned. Had he said it? Was he having one of

his daft moments? His hand was up, waving. He was smiling.

The conductor was lifting my bags on. He helped me up. I got on and went into a car and took my seat and looked out the window.

He sat there in his chair, a little old man, frail and smiling. But I could see tears coming down his face. Mrs. Ebie leaned over to say something. He shook his head.

The train lurched and started. I waved again at them. My family in Lowell. Then I was moving.

Past the mills, where at this very moment all my friends were toiling. And in front, the canopied shops I'd run by that night in terror, with Nicholas pursuing me. I'd never been on a train before. Did life really slide by us like that? Or did you have to be on a train to note it?

Then the back of the Congregational Church. And across the street, my great-grandfather's house.

Oh, I saw it, I saw it, I did! I closed my eyes. I wanted it to be the last thing I saw, leaving Lowell. The blue door.

Author's Note

The quilt has come home! At long last. Brought home by Amanda, granddaughter of Abigail, who, in *A Stitch in Time*, the first book in the Quilt Trilogy, ran off with a Southerner right under her father's nose. Her father, of course, being Nathaniel Chelmsford, who was a mean and bitter man back in 1788, and who allowed the hurts and betrayals of the past, real and imagined, to break his family apart.

Amanda was told by her aging grandmother, more than half a century after the quilt was divided by the three sisters — Abigail, Hannah and Thankful — to bring her part back North and piece it together with the rest.

In this, the third book of the trilogy, Amanda does more than that. She not only brings the last remaining piece of the quilt home; she survives a shipwreck, eludes a would-be killer, and, like Walking Breeze in *Broken Days*, the second quilt book, she loses her piece of the quilt before it can identify her, so she is rejected by Nathaniel

Chelmsford. Turned away by her great-grand-father. Forced to make it on her own. Just like Walking Breeze.

Are family curses handed down? Amanda comes to think they are. Like Walking Breeze, she goes to work in her great-grandfather's mill, forced into labor along with the other mill girls, because she is left penniless. Because everyone says she is dead.

Only now in 1841 the little mill in Beverly, where Walking Breeze first worked, has turned into the booming, bustling mills in the complex at Lowell. During her tenure there, Amanda not only meets some of the more colorful girls who work in the mill, but she gets in on the ground floor of the first labor movement in America.

When Amanda meets Walking Breeze, who now calls herself Nancy and is in charge of the print works, the quilt comes home in more ways than one. Nancy needs a new design for fabric. Amanda needs the ten-hour movement petition signed, because she wants to fulfill a promise she made to her grandmother "to help people when the power to do so is given to you."

Amanda has a design. Fresh, new. What design? From a bird her grandfather Nate drew on the back of a letter to her grandmother years ago, while his ship dropped anchor off the Canary Islands. The same bird featured in the centerpiece of Abigail's quilt.

Amanda trades Grandfather Nate's design for

Nancy's signature (and that of all her girls) on the petition to help make life better for hundreds of mill workers.

The deal is struck. Nancy and Amanda make friends. And Nate Videau's bird is a hot new calico design for the print works in the mill of the man who refused to let Nate marry his daughter, years before.

Nate Videau would have loved the irony of it. So would Thankful, Nancy's mother, who had been stolen by Indians in *A Stitch in Time*. So would Jemmy, who came up to visit his estranged family in *Broken Days*, met Walking Breeze (before she called herself Nancy), and wanted to help her be received into the family.

Now Jemmy's niece comes to bring the quilt home. Jemmy was killed fighting in the War of 1812, and was so lionized by his mother Abigail, that Amanda's father, — Jemmy's younger brother — is a failure. Amanda is sent North by that father, because he needs a better price for his cotton. And her ninety three year old great grand father, Nathaniel Chelmsford, agrees to buy the cotton, if she comes along with it.

Does life come full circle? I believe it does. And this is the point of my Quilt Trilogy. I also believe that everything we do in life affects those around us and those who follow us. I have seen it in my own life. I wanted my readers to see it in this trilogy.

I also wanted them to follow the teenage characters in *A Stitch in Time*, to care about them and wonder what happened to them. Well, they grew up. There they are, the grown-ups in *Broken Days*, with a whole set of oddities and quirks that the teens of that book cannot understand. Can teens ever understand their elders? Then, in *The Blue Door*, the teens of *Broken Days* have grown up. They are the older generation. My readers learn what happened to the teens in *A Stitch in Time*. They have matured, led full lives and died.

This is the effect I wanted to achieve in my multigenerational trilogy. I wanted to give my young readers a sense of *having lived all those years with my characters, seen them grow up, affect each other, and pass on.*

I decided to place the third book in 1841 because it was the year of the first stirrings of the labor movement in America, the year the girls in Lowell were circulating their ten-hour petition.

This was also the time frame in which I found so many "movers and shakers" amongst the young women of Lowell: girls like Lucy Larcom, Harriot Curtis, and Lizzy Turner, who wrote for the *Lowell Offering*, the now-famous literary magazine that carried the writings of those who toiled all day in the mills.

The years 1841–42 were also the period in which *The Operatives Magazine*, also written by mill girls, was published. The first strike in Lowell, called a "turn-out," happened before then, in October 1836, when one of the operatives "stood on a pump and gave vent to the feelings of her companions in a neat speech, declaring that it was their duty to resist all attempts at cutting down the wages." It was also one of the first strikes of cotton factory operatives that ever took place in this country.

I made Plumy, a fictitious character in the book, the one who gave that speech a little over four years before Amanda arrives. She is therefore tagged a troublemaker.

Which brings me to the real purpose of the author's note, to separate fact from fiction.

With the exception of Lucy Larcom, Lizzy Turner, Clementine Averill, and Harriot Curtis, who actually worked in the mills and were activists at this time, just about everyone else in the book is made up. But all my fictional characters have roles and motivations rooted in history. They carry the cultural baggage of those who lived at the time.

Railroads (or the cars, as they were called) were few and far between. Steamboats were popular. But dangerous. The accident in my book is based on no particular mishap, but was a common occurrence.

In 1841, slavery in the South was in full bloom. Northerners, especially New Englanders, were disparaging slaveholders, who were, in turn, attacking the North for the plight of the mill girls. The issue of "chattel slavery versus wage slavery" was waged in newspapers and parlors. Yet, while they criticized the Southern slaveholders, the owners of the Northern mills and those who benefited from them could not have done without the South's cotton. Or the system from which it originated.

The mill girls came to Lowell for various reasons: to make money to support those at home; to send brothers through college; to gain independence for the first time in their lives; to get away from backwater towns where there was no culture. Many hid out from bad marriages and abusive husbands in the mills, like Elinora. Many contracted bad coughs or illnesses, had to go home, and died. Many were injured and even killed on the job. Many became educated and went on to do better things. Or married and used their money for dowries.

Amanda's father's plantation, on St. Helena's Island off the coast of South Carolina, is based on Tombee, from the book *Tombee: Portrait of a Cotton Planter*. By studying *Tombee*, which is the journal of Thomas B. Chaplin, I learned about the culture, moods, agriculture, social life, weather, traditions, problems, and lifestyles of the planters on St. Helena's Island.

In *Broken Days*, I planted the germ of an idea. Jemmy tells Ebie about the blue doors on the slaves' houses on St. Helena's Island, blue doors that keep away hants (ghosts). Blue doors painted with the paint from old indigo pots.

Amanda is very mindful of the blue doors on the slave cabins on her father's plantation. And their significance. Blue is a lucky color for her. Her father makes little blue pills to remedy ills. They are his talisman. Then, when Amanda comes North, she is startled to see the blue door on her great-grandfather's house. Ebie had the door painted blue. Ebie who, as a teen in *Broken Days*, fell in love with her cousin Jemmy.

Then, when Amanda finds a blue door on the Print Works at the mill, the connection is picked up, like an unraveled thread, to be tied to all the loose threads, the questions she brought in her mind from home.

As in all my books, there are hundreds of historical facts in this novel. If they seem casually presented, that is my intent. They are meant to be interwoven. Just like the threads in the quilt that Amanda brings home, fifty-three years after her grandmother ran away with her piece of it.

Home. Where we all find our answers, if we look hard enough. And where, if we look even harder, we all find the answers to ourselves.

And now, in *The Blue Door*, I've brought the three pieces of the quilt home to be made into one; when Amanda returns, when Nancy returns, so they, with Ebie, can stitch it together as Hannah, Abigail, and Thankful started to do so many years ago.

Bibliography

Cunliffe, Marcus. *Chattel Slavery and Wage Slavery: The Anglo-American Context, 1830–1860.* Athens, Georgia: The University of Georgia Press, 1979.

Drago, Harry Sinclair. *The Steamboaters: From the Early Sidewheelers to the Big Packets.* New York, N.Y.: Dodd Mead & Company, 1967.

Ewen, William H. *Days of the Steamboats.* New York, N.Y.: Parents Magazine Press, 1967.

Hoyt, Edwin P. *American Steamboat Stories.* New York, N.Y.: Abelard-Schuman, 1966.

The Lowell Offering: Writings by New England Mill Women, 1840–1845. New York, N.Y.: J.B. Lippincott, Co., 1977.

Robinson, Harriet H. *Loom and Spindle.* Kailua, Hawaii: Press Pacifica, 1976.

Rosengarten, Theodore. *Tombee: Portrait of a Cotton Planter, With the Plantation Journal of Thomas B. Chaplin, 1822–1890.* New York, N.Y.: William Morrow, 1986.

Zaroulis, Nancy. *Call the Darkness Light.* New York, N.Y.: Doubleday, Inc., 1979.

About the Author

ANN RINALDI is one of today's best-known writers of historical fiction for young adults. She is the author of six ALA Best Books for Young Adults, including *In My Father's House* and *Wolf by the Ears*, winner of the 1994 Pacific Northwest Library Association Young Reader's Choice Award, Senior Division, and one of the 100 "Best of the Best" ALA Best Books for Young Adults of the last 25 years. Ms. Rinaldi is also the recipient of an award from the DAR for her historical fiction.

Ann Rinaldi lives in Somerville, New Jersey, with her husband.